Hey Harry, Hey Matilda

Hey Harry, Hey Matilda

Rachel Hulin

Doubleday

New York London Toronto Sydney Auckland

www.doubleday.com

DOUBLEDAY and the portrayal of an anchor with a dolphin are registered trademarks of Penguin Random House LLC.

Grateful acknowledgment is made to the following for permission to reprint previously published material:

Cody Curran: Excerpt from "When I Saw You," lyrics by Cody Curran. Reprinted by permission of the author.

Douglas Music Corp: Excerpt from "Jewish and Goyish" by Lenny Bruce. Reprinted by permission of Douglas Music Corp c/o Don Williams Music Group, Inc. 9425 Santa Ana Rd. Ventura, CA 93001.

Nadia N. Sawicki: Excerpt from "Sixteen" and "Seventeen (You Wore Blue)" by Nadia N. Sawicki, copyright © 1997 by Nadia N. Sawicki. Reprinted by permission of the author.

Jacket design by Emily Mahon
Jacket photograph © Rachel Hulin

Library of Congress Cataloging-in-Publication Data

Names: Hulin, Rachel, author.
Title: Hey Harry, hey Matilda : a novel / Rachel Hulin.
Other titles: Hey Harry | Hey Matilda
Description: First edition. | New York : Doubleday, 2017.
Identifiers: LCCN 2016017745 (print) | LCCN 2016031567 (ebook) | ISBN 9780385541671 (hardback) | ISBN 9780385541688 (ebook)
Subjects: LCSH: Twins—Fiction. | Brothers and sisters—Fiction. | Secrets—Fiction. | BISAC: FICTION / Contemporary Women. | FICTION / Family life. | GSAFD: Bildungsromans. | Epistolary fiction.
Classification: LCC PS3608.U424 H49 2017 (print) | LCC PS3608.U424 (ebook) | DDC 813/.6—dc23
LC record available at https://lccn.loc.gov/2016017745

MANUFACTURED IN THE UNITED STATES OF AMERICA

1 2 3 4 5 6 7 8 9 10

First Edition

To David

Part One: September

Hey Harry,

Today was kind of a wash. I spent fifteen minutes on hold with my bank before I pounded enough 00000000s into the phone to connect me to a real person. I was convinced this fraudulent entity called SBUX on my statement was slowly and erroneously taking money out of my account in $4 and $5 increments. I was extremely put out that I had to spend my time dealing with this. I was really outraged.

It turns out SBUX is Starbucks. I had to hang up on the customer service lady because she was being smug.

Unrelated: Did you know "Pomeranian" is an adjective referring to Pomerania, an area divided between Poland and Germany? Maybe that's why Pomeranians look so much like Grandma.

.

Hey Matilda,

Life is logistics. You've got to learn to deal with these daily annoyances, Mat. You're too hard done by.

Me, I make lists. You should make a list each morning and then follow it carefully.

.

Hey Harry,

I just put three hundred Christmas lights (so cheap off-season!) on a tree that's barely three feet high. If I look at it and then look away quickly, little dots swim across my field of vision. It's pretty excellent. In other news, the lady across the street keeps her blinds about twelve inches raised, so that when she's just out of the shower and her lights are on, I can see the swath of her upper thigh to her lower abdomen, and her pubic hair is a wild, distracting show. It's like the classic '70s pubic hair that you just don't see anymore.

The Brazilian bikini wax craze has had a really pervasive and detrimental effect on vaginas, Harry. This kind of thing is a rare occurrence.

Needless to say, I'm tremendously visually inspired right now. What's new with you?

(Don't tell Mom about the tree.)

.

Hey Matilda,

Two resounding thoughts from my weekend.

One: There was a woman in the newspaper saying she doesn't like French-kissing. This has caused problems in her marriage, but she just can't bring herself to do it. I feel somewhat vindicated by this. But I won't say I told you so.

Two: I watched basketball for a while on TV and had the realization that fouls are bad, not good! You don't actually want to make them. That clears some things up for me about seventh-grade gym.

Anyway, that's all for today—I'm off to grade some disappointing papers.

.

Hey Harry,

I don't remember you telling me you don't like French-kissing, but I'll let you tacitly tell me so. I just got home and these were the contents of my mailbox, so I made a list. I don't like what this says about me, it doesn't seem true.

A. Two Ivy League alumni magazines
B. Two *New Yorker*s
C. Two *New York* magazines
D. One *Economist* magazine
E. Two artist residency rejections

Then I had to have some bourbon.

.

Hey Matilda,

The boyfriend reads the *Economist*? I give you two seven more months at the outside.

I'm sorry you've forgotten that I don't like kissing, but I'm sure you do remember that I like to get all my important correspondence out to folks on Tuesday mornings, as that's when they're most likely to read and respond. Tuesday between 10 and 11 a.m. After coffee, before lunch haze. So hopefully I have your full attention right now.

I think you're having bad luck, to be sure, with this residency stuff, but I also think your energy isn't in the right place. I just read this great book called *Flow: The Psychology of Optimal Experience.* It teaches how, by ordering the information that enters our consciousness, we can discover true happiness and greatly improve the quality of our lives.

Try it, M. Here are some chapter headers:

The Waste of Free Time
The Rules of the Games of the Mind
Flow through the Senses: The Joys of Seeing
Disorder in Consciousness: Psychic Entropy

Now go *make some work*! Make, make, create! Don't analyze it, and don't yell at bank operators.

Also: I saw an undergrad with a bowl cut and high striped socks on campus today, and it reminded me of you in your field hockey glory. You know, sports are a flow activity, too.

One more thing, Matilda—bird-watching is also a flow activity. You can get iBird Explorer for your mobile device. Then you can identify birds.

And lay off the bourbon, please.

·

Hey Harry,

Great tip on the bird-watching. Remind me again when I'm fifty and live in backwoods Maine.

And keep your eyes off those coeds.

·

Hey Matilda,

I remembered where I got the bit about creating and not analyzing—from John Cage's Rules for Students and Teachers:

Rule #8: Do not try to create and analyze at the same time. They are different processes.

Do you know what rule #9 is?

Rule #9: Be happy whenever you can manage it. Enjoy yourself. It is lighter than you think.

I tell this one to my students all the time.

.

Hey Harry,

#9 is a made-up lie. Do your students call you on it?

I fell asleep with my headphones on last night. I woke up with my music still blaring, in a cold sweat. The lyrics I woke up to were about terror and stagnation:

You don't really care about the trials of tomorrow
Rather lay awake in a bed full of sorrow

Do you ever feel like the universe is giving us hints about our future all the time but we're unable to understand?

.

Hey Matilda,

I think these signs happen more often to you than to the rest of us.

.

Hey Harry,

I think you're right. I get the signs but not the message. I'm like a highly attuned, extremely useless oracle. I'm surprised you're lacking this ability, Harry. Our twin genome is failing you. I wish we were exactly the same, but you got that pesky Y.

Guess what? I found out today the head of my old grad school art program has retired and taken a job as a real estate broker. Compared to that, wedding photography doesn't seem so bad. At least it's a stone's throw from actual art. A groom even told me last week "don't hesitate to be artistic."

.

Hey Matilda,

It could definitely be worse. I like to remind myself that teaching writing is highly related to actual writing.

.

Hey Harry,

Yes, teaching writing is perhaps the gateway to writing! You should probably write something, though, to prove the rule.

.

Matilda,

Oh, I'm writing all the time. Just mostly in my head.

.

Harry,

If I looked on the bright side, my thinking would go like this: It's a good thing that I accidentally grabbed the laxatives instead of the ibuprofen this morning, because now my system is cleaner than it has ever been at 3 p.m. on a Wednesday, and I can eat some extra veggie burger because I've cleared room for it.

If I looked on the dark side, my thinking would go like this: This bride thinks I'm a drugged-out freak because I keep running to the bathroom during our business meeting, and not only will I not book this job, but I'll have to skip my dinner date* too because it may be OK to take three ibuprofens but three natural and good-for-you laxative tablets take a full twenty-four hours to churn through.

*Which was my idea to bring romance back into my relationship and now will seem like "poor follow-through," one of my major issues, according to him.

You wouldn't believe this bride, Harry. Her name is Catherine and she's marrying someone named William! I think she was affecting a British accent to capitalize on the coincidence. She gave me relationship advice, too. Told me to ditch the boyfriend and wait until I'm ovulating (only she called it being in heat, like a cat, because we're all mammals after all) and then go to an expensive bar with good clientele and wait for men to approach me. She said that hormones always work.

Groundbreaking advice. We ARE all mammals. Mammals who will mate and then die, never to return. Only our spawn will remember us. Until they also die.

.

Hey Matilda,

I just got back from the Poconos for my men's retreat. The Poconos strike me as very Jewish, but the experience was goyish. Far too many Utz and Kraft products were being bandied about. Remember the Lenny Bruce thing from the seventies? Here it is in case you forgot.

Jewish and Goyish

Dig: I'm Jewish. Count Basie's Jewish. Ray Charles is Jewish. Eddie Cantor's goyish. B'nai B'rith is goyish; Hadassah, Jewish.

If you live in New York or any other big city, you are Jewish. It doesn't matter even if you're Catholic; if you live in New York, you're Jewish. If you live in Butte, Montana, you're going to be goyish even if you're Jewish.

Kool-Aid is goyish. Evaporated milk is goyish even if the Jews invented it. Chocolate is Jewish and fudge is goyish. Fruit salad is Jewish. Lime Jell-O is goyish. Lime soda is very goyish.

All Drake's Cakes are goyish. Pumpernickel is Jewish and, as you know, white bread is very goyish. Instant potatoes, goyish. Black cherry soda's very Jewish, macaroons are very Jewish.

Underwear is definitely goyish. Balls are goyish. Titties are Jewish.

Celebrate is a goyish word. Observe is a Jewish word. Mr. and Mrs. Walsh are celebrating Christmas with Major Thomas Moreland, USAF (ret.), while Mr. and Mrs. Bromberg observed Hanukkah with Goldie and Arthur Schindler from Kiamesha, New York.
—Lenny Bruce

PS Why don't people say "dig" anymore? I'm going to take it up.

·

Hey Harry,

I feel like you need to be fifty and just off your second failed marriage before you even consider going on a men's retreat, but we've been over this.

I do like Lenny Bruce. If I'm not mistaken, he is dead like all the good poets and artists and the rest of us (eventually). I've made a Jewish and goyish version of this in honor of my brides:

Dig: I'm Jewish. Tents are Jewish, banquet halls, goyish.

If you make a long toast, give wet lipstick kisses, or have chair dancing at your wedding, you're Jewish. If you're married in Newport, RI, you're going to be goyish even if you're Jewish.

Fondant icing is goyish. Manischewitz is goyish even though the Jews invented it. Prosecco is Jewish and champagne is goyish. Seltzer is Jewish. Jägermeister is goyish. Shots of Jäger are very goyish.

All veils are goyish. Pantyhose are Jewish. Stockings are Jewish. (But if you call them nylons, they're goyish.) Bridesmaids are goyish. Maids of honor, Jewish. Ring bearers are goyish, dog ring bearers very goyish.

Sobbing fathers are all Jews. Mothers dabbing their eyes are goyish. Bands are Jewish. DJs are goyish, even if they play Paul Simon.

Vests are definitely goyish. Bow ties are Jewish. Garter belts, Jewish.

"Wedding" is goyish. "Marriage" is Jewish.

Film is Jewish. Digital: goyish. Video: extremely goyish.

Mr. and Mrs. John Paul Bradley are pleased to announce the wedding of their children.

Mr. Max Hirsch and Mrs. Rose Beckerman request the honor of your presence at the marriage of their daughter.

·

Hey Matilda—

Well done.

·

Hey Harry,

Thanks. You know I enjoy praise from the internet.

I think I'll purchase www.praisefromtheinternet.com and each day put up an encouraging thought. E.g.:

Good job!
Keep going!

You have exceptionally nice hair and teeth.
Da Vinci was underrecognized once, too.

Wouldn't that be good for the world?

.

Hey Matilda,

It would be. I might add:

There's still time to be famous!
You'll definitely get tenure, don't give it a moment's thought!

.

Hey Harry,

Home-front malaise. I painted the hallway a delightful buttercup yellow this weekend, and Nate showed not the slightest interest in joining in the improvements. Haven't you seen the paint commercials? The dads and boyfriends ALWAYS help. They LEAD, even.

.

Hey Matilda,

I'm always surprised when I see the undergrads on campus moving into their dorms with diligent fathers towing their dressers and duffels. Seems like an alternate world of responsible men, it's quite foreign. Speaking of, have you heard from him lately?

.

Hey Harry,

Oh yes, we had our quarterly email exchange about death and futility.

.

Hey Matilda,

Share please.

.

Hey Harry,

Hi Matilda! I was just looking at a picture of a retirement home on the seashore. I imagined myself there in 30 years. I'll be almost 95. Then I thought, "Wow, Matilda will be 62!" I imagined you as aged as I am now. Then I had to write to you— before you get any older!

I was moved by our conversation a few months back at Grandma's. It was deep—psychologically and spiritually. Love, death, the possibility of human choice in our lives. We were on the same wavelength. I said how choosing one path meant we lost forever all the other possibilities foregone. You said, "Yeah, it's like dying!" When I thought back later on this, I laughed heartily. I recognized your response as what I often say as well. It's genetic! Amazing, and wonderful. I'm so happy you are alive on this earth!!!

.

Hey Matilda,

Ah, that's a good one, thanks.

.

Hey Harry,

Yep.

Also: why is it so cold outside?

I've been a little aimless of late, or maybe just distracted by the nippy air. I don't want to put on pants again. I can't leave the house.

I need to locate the midpoint between a loafer and a boot. What are you up to?

.

Hey Matilda,

Nothing much doing here. Grading papers. I went ahead and bought that online genetic test I told you about—the price went down to $99, so I figured it was worth it. It will give the part of me that was good at high school biology a little thrill, I think.

It's pretty amazing what science can tell us about our ancestry now. I'm so curious to imagine what our forebears were up to—maybe it's the writer in me, but I find it totally fascinating. It's so odd that most people don't know anything about even two generations back.

.

Hey Harry,

That just shows you how quickly our own grandchildren will cease to give two shits about us. Maybe that's why Grandma is so intense.

Will this test tell you if you (but mostly I) will die early of cancer? I maintain a lingering and not-insignificant fear that I will die early of Mother's breast cancer, or will it be Grandpa's Alzheimer's? If I start thinking too much about it I can't breathe right.

You know—I don't even know my blood type, which is a tragedy because I can't do the blood-type diet. Although periodically I read the rules of each diet and decide which one *sounds* like me and then I fantasize about the diet I should be on to give me lots of energy and lifepurpose™. I think I should be B-type blood, because those are the folks who can eat cheese, lots of it.

.

Hey Matilda,

My blood type is A. I seriously doubt yours is B, unless you secretly hail from India. And yes, the genetics test tells you the likelihood of getting all types of diseases, and also tells you how much of which ethnicity you have in your ancestry. I will share the results with you—ours would probably be very similar, except different traits show up on the male/female chromosomes.

I'm not so interested in the diseases part. Carpe diem, right? Try not to stop breathing. Mom's was a tiny lump.

.

Harry,

Genetics are a bitch. I see this often when I'm shooting weddings, during the family portrait (aka hell) portion of the event. Five beautiful, vivacious daughters and two troll-like, blustery sons. In any case, I hope you get some exciting news about the future.

It's amazing, Harry, that you can find this genetic stuff out from spitting in a tube and sending it to a website. I knew things were going to get good after they invented the Walkman.

.

Harry,

It's kind of a gray day today, so I've been image-searching Suprematist paintings and redrawing them to make me feel better. The whole movement was based on "the supremacy of pure artistic feeling," so I think if I re-create them, then I also can have a pure artistic feeling.

(I always thought that temp job archiving slides of Russian art from the early 1900s was just going to be a minimum-wage throwaway!)

Here is a handmade Rodchenko that's about me and you. A Fakechenko. Do you love it?

.

Matilda,

Who is big and who is little?

.

Harry,

I am big.

.

Matilda,

Seems about right—you up on the pedestal, me grounding you.

.

Harry,

You taking credit, me slightly off-kilter. Speaking of—I don't like this new feeling I'm having lately, the feeling of oldness. I know someday soon I'll wake up and realize I'm absolutely irrelevant and it will be terrifying. Or maybe I'm there already, Harry.

.

Hey Matilda,

Don't worry, we're not old. It's all just beginning to crystallize. Whenever I start to feel old, I think of a painful moment in my early twenties, and I feel so relieved to be past that. I also look at my students, who are so clueless, and realize I know more than I think I do. Today I had to explain to most of my English Lit I section who Virginia Woolf was. Help me out, high school English teachers! The kids they're sending me are so half formed.

.

Hey Harry,

It takes a long time for humans to understand things, give them a break. For example: I remember when I thought Mondale-Ferraro was one person. And I just wanted Mom to stop talking about him.

By the way, what *was* the most painful moment of your twenties?

.

Hey Mat,

Hmm. Probably when I confessed to Dad that I was doing too many drugs at college and he asked me for the number of my dealer. So that he could "take that cocaine finally." That was disappointing. You?

.

Hey Harry,

Well, let me tell you the story about Martha's Vineyard, Harry. As I recall you were in Nepal on a yak and missed the whole thing.

It started when I answered an ad in the campus newspaper. It said:

Come to Martha's Vineyard for the summer. Stay in our family's mansion for free. Drink our chocolate liqueur while we're not there, and drive our Jeep around the island with abandon. Collect $300 a week and schtup the pool boy. In return, fold some towels and help us make tuna sandwiches. (Celery, no crusts.)

Well OK! I said. That is a king's ransom. Sign me right up. I was nursing a mild heartbreak anyway—Max, remember him from freshman year? "I want to see other people," he had said. "I feel too young to be officially entangled," he said (after pursuing me relentlessly all fall semester).

This was a big house, the biggest in Edgartown. A white Greek Revival situation with a huge sloping mahogany staircase that led you to bedrooms you referred to by color. "And you will be staying in the blue room this week, Mrs. Fancie." The family entertained a lot of guests when they were in town, which was sporadically.

When the family was there the sheets were turned down each night, a chocolate mint placed on the pillow. The toilet paper was folded to a point and rolled *over,* not *under.*

There were five of us crowded into the maid area of four rooms clustered in a dormer over the kitchen. No AC, just fans in every room that whirred loudly all day and all night and put the warm-air smell of expensive dinner into our clothes.

We answered the phone not with our names, but with a number: "5510, can I help you?" We had on khaki shorts and white knit polo shirts from Lands' End that had been bought for us to wear, and we looked like squares, the shape. The blond-haired, ruddy, formerly handsome chef drank twelve Bud Lights in cans every afternoon in quick succession, and you could tell from the color of his eyes that Bud Light in bulk is *not good for you*. He was not fond of me at all.

The two girls we were working with had deep tans they slathered on from a pink bottle and really long fake fingernails. They snuck boys into the dormer and rarely included me in their conversations. But if they had liked me I would have liked them.

My favorite family member was the youngest daughter, who was glamorous and untouchable when I picked her up from the airport.

She would come back to the serving area in between courses and we'd smoke menthols and drink malt liquor together. Her name was Martina and she had dramatic yelling fights with her father that echoed through the house at night. She made "dad" into five syllables. "D-a-a-a-d!" High-pitched. She always had a fresh manicure, with black glossy polish ten or so years before black was all the edgy rage. I opened her diet sodas by the pool and handed them to her. She didn't want to pop the cans herself.

Max came to visit on the Fourth of July weekend. His eyes looked especially blue and he was talking about other girls. Older girls, girls with accents. I think he thought I was over him. He was of course unindoctrinated in the ways of being the help so he kept making the mistake of wandering into the main house and nearly fraternizing with the family.

"Do you think I have a chance with Martina?" he kept asking me.

And then he'd finish the champagne that had been left out and gone flat.

I went to sleep early one night after my run, tired and keyed up from the asthma medication I'd been popping to look less rhomboid in my maid outfit. When I stepped into the blinding morning sun the next day to skim the leaves from the surface of the water I saw two bathing suits mingling together, Max's and Martina's, four feet down on the dappled, watery pool bottom, and I sat down and cried.

At the end of the summer the girls with the fake tans had a blowout fight because it turned out they were secret bisexual lovers and were having a jealousy thing.

Which proved I didn't know anything about anything. *That* was the worst moment of my twenties. I got it right out of the way at the beginning of the decade.

I missed you, Harry. You should have come to see me.

.

Hey Matilda,

I remember you after that summer. Skinny and cold in eighty degrees. Hair standing up on your arm like a mole-type creature.

I never liked that Max. Didn't he turn out to be gay?

.

Harry,

No. He married a mayonnaise heiress. So now, presumably, he has all the champagne he needs. And more tuna salad sandwiches than he can ever eat. Isn't it odd how marriage can still completely change your fortunes and make your friends envyhate you forever?

I should call them up.

Matilda,

Top three ironic tattoos in my classroom today:

1. Anchor
2. MOM & DAD
3. Finger mustache

.

Harry,

Do you know anything about this Zelda game? Is Zelda a boy or a girl?

.

Matilda,

Does your boyfriend make you watch him play video games? I give you two five more months, max.

.

Harry,

It's not so bad. I sit on the couch with the cat and stare at the canary-yellow projection of POLLO that comes through the window onto the wall from the twenty-four-hour bodega next door. I pretend it's a personal Barbara Kruger installation telling me to have organic free-range chicken fingers for dinner. And then I make some, and I dip them in BBQ sauce and they are delicious.

Nate has a good friend named Amit who is always over. I used to resent it, but now I find the dynamic of three people actually sort of useful. It keeps things a bit varied, and you can't be *quite* so passive-aggressive when your boyfriend refuses to paint your apartment walls yellow to coordinate with the bodega sign.

Amit works for an insurance company, on the bad-guy side, and makes loads of dough, so he buys us beer for penance. He is amusing, Harry. He wraps himself in the gauzy curtains when the lights are off, so that the yellow from the bodega filters through them in a canary-gold color, and he pretends he's onstage and sings. Usually he's Freddie Mercury.

Left alone with big fat Fanny, she was such a naughty nanny

My god, that Freddie got away with murder!

·

Hey Matilda,

I think maybe you should kick your boyfriend standards up just a touch.

·

Harry,

I think maybe you should trust the universe enough to attempt a real relationship.

·

Matilda,

I'm patient, you see.

.

Harry,

In any case, I kind of like Nate's boldness. The first night we went out, he bragged that he was broke, declared to the bartender "I'll take your cheapest swill, sir!" and asked me to pay.

Ballsy, right? And at the time he was an intern, but NOW— associate editor.

.

Matilda,

Truly impressive.

.

Harry,

I've been thinking so much about the Large Hadron Collider today. It's an enormous machine in Switzerland that is supposed to answer the mysteries of time and space and some other things, more or less.

And I read an article today saying that someone has been found near the collider, claiming to be from the future!! It's about time, too. Because if no one has come from the future yet, then time travel must be impossible, if you think about it.

I 100% believe this time traveler. He makes me very happy.

In other news, I have a glamorously located pimple that makes me feel like Marilyn Monroe. Hopefully it will stick around for another few days.

·

Matilda,

The date on the article you linked to is April 1. So . . . I think your time traveler may be a hoax.

·

Harry,

Fuck.

·

Matilda,

If it makes you feel any better—maybe no one has come from the future yet because time is not linear at all but more like a Möbius strip, so that we're all really living at the same time, despite the perception that we die and are born in order throughout time. Just a thought.

·

Harry,

Maybe that's why Steve Jobs said "Oh wow. Oh wow. Oh wow" when he died. That would make sense. Although I doubt there's a big reveal right away. Unless time immediately stretches out upon death's door.

.

Hey Matilda,

Einstein said, "The only reason for time is so that everything doesn't happen at once."

BTW, I'm going to start checking my email only twice a day, at 9 a.m. and again at 4 p.m. I'm starting to have feelings of panic when I'm out of range.

.

Harry,

Technology has truly ruined all of our lives. All day we stare at computerized screens, caress them, feel beholden. I doubt you can pare down your email consumption that much, though. We're Goodmans. We are addictive by nature.

.

Matilda,

I am pretty good at fighting these addictive urges, however.

.

Hey Harry,

Pro tip: It's more fun to just give in.

Hey Matilda,

It may be more fun for now, but it won't be in the long run.

.

Hey Harry,

That is where we differ. You're the long-distance runner. I'm a sprinter. In my defense, it's the city that's my enabler.

The thing about living here—you're always on the edge of being broke, or downsized, or apartment searching. You're perpetually on a forty-five-minute train ride somewhere, from which you need to return in the dark.

Fall is too short, and is primarily spent worrying about winter. And once winter arrives, it's better to stay in bed, with small breaks taken for the Laundromat, where you'll need to protect your underwear from hipsters and vagrants.

One time Grandma came to visit me here at Mom's insistence and asked me when I'm "going to live like a normal person." She was appalled at my lack of a dishwasher, among many other things, notably a promising partner. And deep down, so am I.

SO am I, Harry.

.

Matilda,

Perhaps you could consider another locale?

Harry,

Don't act crazy. It's my destiny to live this way.

.

Matilda,

Suit yourself.

Today I got to class and I did not have my phone in my pocket, or my glasses on my head. One step forward, two steps back, I guess.

(It's odd, because I don't leave the house without saying "Spectacles, testicles, wallet, and watch" first. I always say it, I can't help myself.)

.

Harry,

I say, "Phoneries, ovaries, wallet, and keys."

.

Matilda,

You must misplace your glasses often, then.

.

Hey Harry,

I got another bride today, for June. She showed me her invitations. Two little swallows in the corner of manila cardstock, holding trumpets and greenery in their tiny beaks, proclaiming the wedding date proudly to all the guests.

What is it with brides and birds, Harry? What's so romantic about birds? Aren't they harbingers of disease? Don't they go to the bathroom on our heads?

Is it because they fly around?

.

Hey Matilda,

I don't know. I think swans are nice and emblematic for weddings because they come from ugly ducklings. Evolution of self, etc. etc.

.

Hey Harry,

Unless the ugly duckling just turns into a goose and then has its liver removed. But good point.

I think penguins would be a more apt wedding bird, because they mate for life. From now on, I'm going to call my brides "birds." It feels nice to do that. You should come up with a name for your students, too.

.

Matilda,

I think I will call them bats. Fumbling around in the dark, alighting on false inspirations.

.

Harry,

I've realized something.

I have four main moods:

Depressive-Depressive: I am sad and things are pointless and I am going to nap.
Aggressive-Depressive: I am sad and it is your fault and I am going to nap.
Depressive-Hyper: I am sad and things are pointless but let's have some beers and jump around.
Aggressive-Hyper: I am sad and it is your fault and I am going to start a fight with you.

.

Hey Matilda—

Do you have a therapist these days?

.

Harry,

I had one, but we just talked all the time about how I resented paying him so much at the end of each session. And of course the whole reason I was in therapy in the first place was because I was so panicked about money.

So then we had sex and went our separate ways.

.

Harry,

Just kidding! About the sex.

.

Matilda,

I wasn't all agape.

.

Harry,

Oh yeah? What would truly shock you? I want you to show some emotion.

BTW: I saw a chart today entitled:

"States Where I Can Live Happily Ever After with My Cousin"

I'm going to send it over to you.

.

Hey Matilda,

Why would you even bring that up?

·

Harry,

It's the **Aggressive-Hyper** talking.

Harry, what's your favorite emotion, and what's your worst?

·

Matilda,

Emotion, or state of being? I like sadness, in its plain old basic state, without any agitation mixed in. I can handle that quite well.

·

Hey Harry,

What about anger? What about rage? Harry, what would make you truly, irretrievably angry with me?

·

Matilda,

OK, just blurt out whatever's bothering you, already. This dance is tiresome.

·

Harry,

I can't, you're far too moral.

Hey Matilda,

Tell me! Lance the boil. I'm not that moral.

·

Harry,

Just remember, Harry: I always have your best interests at heart.

Tell me something about what you're teaching, Harry. Tell me about the bats.

·

Hey Matilda,

I think the seasonal depression is starting to get to you. It creeps up, you know. Get one of those lamps before it's too late.

Since you're asking: I recently gave my writing students an assignment to help them learn to write convincing dialogue. I told them to eavesdrop on a conversation in a public place and write it down, word for word. Here's one I liked. One of my best students *actually stood up and sang it out loud.* What a breath of fresh air. Reminded me of something you would have done!

I don't think Obama would have an infidelity, doesn't seem like
  him
You can kind of tell
Michelle would kill him
This seems like a nice place to have breakfast
Maybe ham and cheese

A croissant
I don't think it would help to wash those pot holders
It's too late
Hmm maybe so
I don't like that Newt
Want a bite of my bagel
Oh this is good
It seems like a type of tropical fruit is in this
Mango?
It was almost four dollars
I need to get some ice
On television last night there was one of Martin Luther King Jr.'s
    daughters
She was talking about some fellow
Said he couldn't have had an affair
How would she know
He does make Domino's pizza
I'm not finished yet
I'm gonna finish
Want to see the **Times***?*
OK
You see the article
Page A6
Sure
Here it is
This thing is all crumpled
Appeared to be a protest against Britain's tough new economic
    sanctions against Iran
They tore down the flag
And burned it
Maybe it's peach?

The other students and I were riveted by the singing. A good day.

·

35

Harry,

I would have done something like that. I was a spectacular
college student, I assure you. I could have gone pro. But then
they forced me into the world.

.

Matilda,

They tried to do that to me, too, but I said, NOPE; PhD.

.

Harry,

I have taken your couch
that was in
Mom's Stock N' Lock

and which you were probably
saving
for someday

forgive me
it was irresistible
so sweet
so pink
and so pungent

.

Matilda,

Was that his idea, to take my couch? I give you two three more months. Also, that assignment isn't until next semester.

.

Harry,

My favorite emotion is shame. Because it's the one I can deal with the least, and the one that comes up the most. Thanks for asking.

.

Matilda,

I didn't need to ask, because I knew that already.

.

Harry,

Oh, well did you know that I've never made myself a sandwich?

.

Matilda,

Yes.

.

Harry,

Say something mean to me so I can react badly.

.

Matilda,

Tomorrow I'll tell you the dream I had and you won't be in it.

.

Harry,

Jerk.

I wrote something for you.

Things I Shouldn't Say Out Loud

"My brother has a nice scrotum." That's going on a list of things I shouldn't say out loud. It will go above "Meat Loaf is my favorite singer" and "I eat cookie dough with raw eggs just to tempt fate."

I should also include "When you told me to give you a compliment, and I said you were smarter than most normal people, that was a lie," and "I don't actually like your cologne, it disgusts me. I don't care if it IS designer."

That's it so far. Maybe I'll think of more later.

Oh! In elementary school I used to pick my nose and then wipe my hand on your pillow. I shouldn't say that either. Also I hate your hair.

Do you like it, Harry?

.

Matilda,

It's not bad.

.

Harry,

Would it kill you to have a personality?

.

Matilda,

I hate your hair, too. And your attitude, which should be improving with age, is deteriorating.

.

Harry,

Yes!!! That's more like it.

Part Two: November

Matilda,

I made a chart, too.

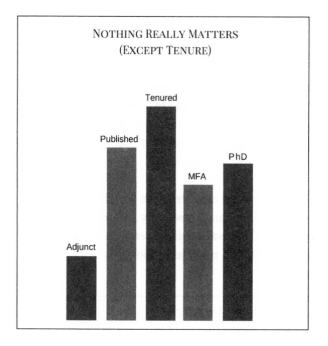

Harry,

Well, having a PhD is not bad, you're third highest on this chart! Perhaps third best is good enough? That seems like a nice motto for life.

Let's distract ourselves from the cruel current world, Harry. Tell me a funny story from our youth.

Hey Matilda,

One time we went to a wedding. We must have been about seven at the time. I was very interested in Transformers, because it was the '80s. The wedding took place at an old camp. It was fall but it was hot, and all the guests wandered about the place with brightly colored drinks in hand. I remember this because we were drinking punch, and you kept cackling "Punch me!" and giggling because you'd had an impossible amount of Hi-C. There were big trees clustered closely together, and if you looked through them, you could see a lake in the distance, but it didn't even look like water, it looked like just a shimmer. The trees had enormous roots that were growing above ground and we put the Transformers and plastic toy ponies on them like totems. We all stayed overnight in little cabins on the property and when we awoke the following day, we walked out onto a still-balmy field strewn with middle-aged bodies in sundresses and suits. And right there among them, sitting and snoring, propped up on a golf cart was Dad, Smirnoff bottle still in hand. "I found him!" you yelled, like you'd won a prize, and ran off to tell Mom.

.

Hey Harry,

Oh, I do remember that. It was one of the only times Mom dressed us alike—you as a sailor with white hat and blue piping, me in a pinafore. Both in bowl cuts. We were positively a sideshow. People were much more charmed by twins back then. Now that there's IVF, it's all old hat.

.

Matilda,

True, twindom felt more special back then. That was a good day.
Mom wasn't even mad at Dad. Maybe she'd just given up by then.

.

Harry,

Or maybe it was a rare day when she could see some humor in
the wreckage of her marriage.

.

Hey Matilda,

Guess what? My genetic test results came back. Pretty much what
you would expect, but still interesting.

Dad's a mutt, which we know. French, English, Irish, German. But
also 2% Native American! That's sort of fascinating to me.

And Mom's a Jew. They don't even qualify it with Polish or Latvian,
they just say: MOTHER: 100% Ashkenazi Jew. They should make
it more interesting, i.e.: FROM THE PALE, very learned.

I do like to consider the most mundane aspects about our
ancestors, Matilda—like, what did they read before bed? Chaucer?

.

Harry,

That's your biggest question? *What did our ancestors read
before bed? Chaucer?!*

Good lord, we're part Native American, I'm going to take horseback-riding lessons and come up with an appropriate name. How about Worried Moon?

You can be Hopeful Bear.

.

Matilda,

I think 2% does not allow us to be culturally insensitive.

.

Harry,

You *would* think that. But we're burying the lead here—what does the disease portion say? Oh god, it makes me so nervous to ask.

.

Matilda,

I already ripped that envelope up, I don't want to know. Why would I want to know? It would ruin my life to know something like that.

.

Harry,

Oh my god, I don't understand you at all! What a wasted opportunity! I NEED TO KNOW!!

.

Matilda,

I think you admire my bravery in the face of the unknown.

.

Harry,

You're not brave because you were spared boobs. You're just lucky.

Worried Moon needs to know the future.

.

Matilda,

Hopeful Bear trusts.

.

Harry,

Ugh, we will have to rectify this.

Speaking of the future . . . Maybe being a wedding photographer isn't all that bad?

I mean—think about it. There is far too little ritual in our culture. Our barren culture doesn't even celebrate death properly.

Weddings are the ultimate ritual, aside from childbirth. And photography is one of the only ways to preserve a moment.

Maybe I should just charge $10,000 a wedding and be a fucking wedding photography boss.

Also, it's such a sociological study I can't stand it.

You can break all the brides down by the kind of fucking dress they wear:

1. SHEATH bride: *Sheaths appear smooth talking, thoughtful, and innocuous at first, but turn high-maintenance when the pressure is on. Sheaths often have very involved parents with money. Sheaths wear straight, tasteful gowns and put gardenias in their hair. They have those little net-type veils that are trying to be chic and traditional without saying "I'm wearing a veil." But they're wearing a veil. They met their husbands in grad school.*

2. A-LINE bride: *What you see is what you get. A-lines don't try too hard or think their wedding is the one moment in life to show what their very essence is about. They allow the bridesmaids to dress themselves and they get married in someone's backyard, at a camp, or in Vermont.*

3. COCKTAIL bride: *Hey, I'm a cocktail bride, I'm doing things a little differently than normal! We might only have appetizers at my wedding! I might wear red! I have a pug and he is my groomsman.*

4. PRINCESS bride: *Fussy, naïve. Confusing choices may include glitter hairspray, Hummer limo, and impractical heels. A hotel venue, matching bridesmaids, and many drunk, red-faced groomsmen. Groom's cake more often than not takes the shape of a state school mascot. Michigan/Wisconsin/Chapel Hill.*

5. MERMAID bride: *Aggressively stylized. Confusing choices are made, generally in the form of a country club venue and a black shirt for the groom. Bride wears a dress that literally* *makes her resemble a fish human. A tremendous level of self-regard and bravery about one's bottom is required.*

·

Matilda,

So what about you? What type would you be? A combination Sheath and A-line?

·

Harry,

No kind, because I can't locate a suitable mate.

·

Matilda,

Well, in that case, I have the answer to your previous riddle.

The midpoint between a loafer and a boot = a clog. Perfect for spinsters!

·

Harry,

Wow, that is correct!

I shall now take clogs out of the "Unacceptable and Just for Mothers Over Fifty-Five" column and will procure a pair as soon as possible.

Matilda,

I imagine you could borrow some from Mom. She has a pair for every occasion. Even waterproof, for the garden and the farmers' market.

·

Hey Harry,

How often do you go over and see her? What do you do for fun out there in the boonies?

·

Matilda,

Well, just last night I went out to dinner at Atomic Wings. And then Mom called and asked me to come fix a broken stair that was keeping her from going to the basement to do laundry, so I swung by on my way home. It was a bigger job than I thought, though, and I finished up late, so I ended up crashing on the couch. But I was totally unable to sleep; the house is really not in great shape. I could hear mice running through the walls all night like we used to hear when we were little, *scratch scratch scratch.* I got up at dawn and went for a run down by the river and then I came home and had a better writing day than I've had in a while.

·

Harry,

That makes me think about how we'd sit in the bath until we were cold prunes listening to Dad's stories about the two heroic mice lost in the woods. What were their names? He had notes on a yellow legal pad; that's the most I ever remember him paying attention to parenting.

Also: There are several things about your last note that raise red flags for me, but I'm going to go straight to my own related mouse story, which coincidentally happened not more than a month ago. Our friend Amit was over, crashing on the couch for the fourth night in a row, because he is twenty-five and I am a too-permissive thirty-something.

So we all went to bed and around 4 a.m. I hear this scraping noise coming from the kitchen. At first I thought it was part of my dream, and then I thought someone was breaking in through the window. So I tiptoe in there and grab a broom on my way (note boldness/braveness) and HOLY SHIT there is a mouse stuck on the glue trap I set. The glue trap that is supposed to be the humane way of killing a mouse is being dragged around the floor, back and forth, and the thing is clearly in distress and it's horrifying and I might be starting to cry a little and then Amit comes in and puts a pot over it and shoos me back to bed. He'll "take care of it in the morning."

Guess who slept through this whole thing?

I don't think Amit should keep sleeping over without a shirt on the couch, it gives me thoughts.

PS The next morning Amit picked up the pot and the mouse was GONE, all that was left was a bunch of hair on the trap and some mouse poo.

PPS Do you think it died?

PPPS Atomic Wings, really?

.

Matilda,

Free-range wings, Matilda, relax. Just because I live in the country doesn't mean I like antibiotics in my meat.

.

Harry,

Really? Because that place was the WORST in high school. So odd, everything is changing without me! I thought that whole town would just be frozen in time from the moment I left.

.

Hey Matilda,

You know what else is odd? Mailmen. For forty-seven cents they will still pick up your letters and bring them to people. Anywhere in the country.

.

Harry,

Yes!! The whole concept of the postal service is INSANE! Sending a missive for less than a dollar!! A deal if you have a forever stamp! It's actually miraculous. Remember our mailman in high school?

·

Matilda,

I do. We'd watch him from the turret when he picked up our letters. They were always addressed back to us, but he'd have to post them anyway. He was a good man, diligent.

·

Harry,

He could have just ignored us, defiled our letters, stuck felonious poo in our box. Anything.

·

Matilda,

He thought we were quite irksome.

·

Harry,

I left him Jolly Ranchers at the holidays to thank him for his kind service. He probably threw them away, which is a shame because they were watermelon—the best flavor.

·

Hey Harry,

1. I heard a song on the radio today which stated that the basis of all love relationships is fear. Do you think that's true? Sadly, I do believe it is.
2. I haven't gone "running" since college. I can't believe you do that every day. If there is one gene you got that I did not, it is the functionality gene.

.

Hey Matilda,

1. Yes. To some extent.
2. My running is your happy hour. We all do what we can.

.

Harry,

ZING.

.

Hey Matilda,

In the bleak landscape of student poetry that is my life, a bright spot comes: I have a promising student. Her name is Vera and she is from Vermont. Actually, her full name is Vivian Remember Parker-Hall, can you believe that? She's an interesting mix of freewheeling and proper. Moneyed but of the people.

On the first day of class I handed out a survey with some basic questions on it and she wrote:

I have two mothers, and I survived Exeter boarding school.

Anything is possible!!!!

Her recent poem was about choosing between having the superhero ability to fly or be invisible. The narrator cannot decide, she is tormented with the choice, and then finally succumbs to a pile of sleeping pills and chooses an endless nap. It was brilliant, though, not overwrought.

.

Harry,

I don't understand the idea of the poem, because of course the only choice is TO FLY!!! Jesus, what is wrong with people? And sleeping pills aren't overwrought?

You're losing your edge, Harry.

Why didn't Mom give me a middle name? I deserve one.

.

Matilda,

Well, I got Angus, so that's cool.

.

Harry,

It's OK. But "Remember"? Be still my heart.

·

Matilda,

It's Puritan, I think. Dad once joked to me that he named me after his favorite Beatle and you after his favorite barmaid.

·

Harry,

That sounds like a classic Dad fabrication. A Dadrication.

·

Matilda,

For the record, I would choose invisibility over flight.

·

Harry,

You confuse me so.

Also, I'm pretty sure I heard that superhero choice posited to folks on the street on the radio. It's not all original, you know.

Unrelated: All the skin on the left side of my body is numb. Do I worry?

·

Matilda,

You could be having a stroke. Take a nap?

.

Harry,

I think I'm numb because I'm frightened again about the passing
of time. How do I slow it down? I've already passed the thrill of a
first kiss, my first taste of caviar, my first swim in the ocean . . . I
have no firsts left! In fact, right now is as good as it's ever going
to get.

.

Matilda,

This is why you're a photographer—you freeze time. And maybe
why I'm a writer—my intense focus when I'm really writing well
makes the clock stop entirely. I have no sense of my own person;
it's just deep, satisfying brain work that turns hours into seconds.
It's not until I close the laptop and look up that I realize that time
has even passed; it's dark outside.

.

Dear Harry,

Why are there commercials for cotton? Who are they trying to
convince?

.

Matilda,

There are also commercials for avocados.

.

Harry,

And pistachios. Though pistachios are $12 at my corner market.

.

Hey Matilda,

That is too many dollars, though lately I find myself craving the excitement and energy of a city. Generally I appreciate the lower standards here. I can leave the house in an old button-down and jeans and still be the best-dressed teacher in the faculty lounge.

.

Harry,

Yes—and you like to be the best. I have no hope of being the best here.

.

Matilda,

I don't thrive on pressure. And all those people everywhere would overload my senses.

.

Hey Harry,

But don't you want your senses to be overloaded? Now's the
time to max them out! We're sitting on a twirling blue speck in
the vast nothingness of space, and we'll be gone before we ever
existed! We may as well flame out. I'm going to, and soon, I can
feel it. Some past missteps are about to catch up with me.

·

Hey Matilda,

You have so much paranoia about impending doom. All things
considered, you lead a charmed life.

·

Harry,

You're not as reasonable as you pretend to be. I'm worried
about the holidays, Harry. About Hanukkah. About coming
home. It's not going to go well. I'm just looking forward to the
New Year, when I can make a list of important herbs and goals
and think very seriously about them and then forget them by
February.

HERBS: ginseng, spirulina, turmeric

GOALS: fame, gratitude, self-respect

·

Hey Matilda,

Do not pre-panic about the holidays.

．

Harry,

It used to be better at this time of year. You were always Mr. Shammes at the Christmas pageant during the token Jewish interlude. I loved that. You lit me on fire.

．

Hey Matilda,

I hated that. Being onstage, in front of a bunch of bored kids—in a flame costume.

．

Hey Harry,

You know, I think about Nazis a lot. Hebrew school scars you for life, watching all of those movies.

．

Matilda,

Sometimes it's good to be reminded that not everyone's on your side.

．

Hey Harry,

I don't need to be reminded of that. I want to focus on joy. I was coming home the other night, on the subway over the river, listening to music on my headphones, full volume. I'd been out for tacos with the boyfriend, but then he'd gone to meet some other friends, so it was just me and Billy Joel's greatest hits, together, on loud and repeat.

And it occurred to me that this feeling of pure happiness—a height and a view, and a head high on tequila and some music of my youth—hasn't happened to me in years. Pure elation. It was nearly spiritual. If they could take out 80% of my brain and leave me with that feeling, I'd have the operation.

How many times does one have that feeling in one's life? Maybe fifteen times, maybe twenty? It was rope-swing-over-a-quarry transcendent.

(I couldn't get out of bed the next day—tequila hangover.)

Billy Joel doesn't seem that much older now than he used to.

.

Hey Matilda,

I think a good way to achieve euphoria, healthily, is through endorphins. Running, yoga, meditation. Those alcohol downswings are not good for you.

.

Hey Harry,

I heard on TV today that they took a great yoga program out of schools in Florida because the Christian parents thought it was religious—saluting the sun and thanking it for life.

Hey Matilda,

Florida seems terrible on a whole lot of levels.

.

Harry,

Here is a new list, about me and you.

Harry—optimist
Matilda—pessimist
Harry—long distance (running, writing)
Mat—sprinter (drinking, relationships)
Harry—invisibility
Matilda—flight

I booked a job the other day, an elusive winter wedding, so I have a bride's deposit. I am going to use $99 of it to buy that genetic test. Now that you've gone and thrown out the answers to WILL I DIE OF DEMENTIA OR MY BOOBS FIRST, I need to take matters into my own hands.

I've been thinking a lot about this. Ruminating. Obsessing maybe a touch.

.

Matilda,

You have been? Be careful about how much you dwell on the future. You're better off creating a narrative of the present.

Harry,

I wrote a short story. It's by me in the future. It's wishful
thinking. Thinking that someday I will get to be pregnant and I
will be married to someone like Captain von Trapp. You probably
never think about babies, but I do. It's my biological imperative.
It's true, we ARE all just mammals. It's not our fault.

<u>Favorite Things</u>

When she was pregnant she was obsessed with Nazi movies. She
started with *Schindler's List* and moved on to *Marathon Man,
Army of Shadows, Au Revoir les Enfants*. She watched them
in bed at night, over eggs in the morning. When she was put on
bed rest for placenta previa in her twenty-eighth week, she took
it as a sign and went full-time. She'd never felt so fulfilled, so
engaged.

Her husband would try to say goodbye in the morning and she'd
hold up her index finger and shake her head, gesturing toward
the TV. *The Sorrow and the Pity*, she mouthed.

The babies came early. They'd expected two girls, but Anne
turned out to have a brother. Her husband looked at his wife
shivering after the C-section, wrapped in blankets, her pallor
yellowish, oxygen in her nose. "Frank is a great name," he said. "I
love it."

Anne, Frank, and their mother stayed in the hospital four days.
She asked her husband to bring the laptop so she could continue
with *Downfall*. The Percocet made her drowsy and emotional;
she couldn't concentrate on the story. Frustrated, she thought
she'd try something else. She played a game: If Anne was

wet, she'd move on to *Nuremberg*. Frank, *Band of Brothers*. Both their diapers were full.

When they got home, her husband surprised her with a freezer full of vegetable lasagna and a DVD of *Enemy at the Gates*. She demolished the béchamel, sighed, and suggested *When Harry Met Sally*.

The summer was exhausting and joyless and, aside from a single moment of passion ignited by an $8 gift bottle of Chardonnay, loveless. They were both surprised when the stick showed a pink strip. He felt light-headed, swore beneath his breath. She smiled for the first time in months and headed for the den. "Where'd you put the remote?" she asked.

But *Triumph of the Will* was boring. *The Pianist* made her sob. She tried *American History X,* turned it off eight minutes in. She hunted for something with Drew Barrymore and told herself to be patient.

Liesl was born after a Julia Roberts marathon. Ten months later came Brigitta, followed by Friedrich and Marta. She was building her own happiness, out of flesh and blood. Bridget Jones cackled in the background. Her husband got a vasectomy.

The years passed quickly as the fame took hold. The children were adorable and loved their dirndls almost as much as the stage. Everyone said she made a great Maria. Even her husband had a new posture. For who wouldn't like being a captain? All was well.

·

Matilda,

Very nice pacing. The end is a little abrupt, but it's tight. Well done!

Harry,

Are you seriously the kind of teacher who just talks about pacing?
What about content? What about interest, life, spark, human
condition! I think I could be a writer, too, you know?

.

Matilda,

Picking a fight? I gave you a compliment. I can tell you more
thoughts later.

.

Harry,

Mom won't let me give my American Girl doll Samantha away to
a seven-year-old I promised it to at a cocktail party. I promised
her, and now I'll break her heart. She's MY doll! When did Mom
commandeer all our childhood things? When we went to college?
I'm really upset about this. Do all belongings revert back to the
landowner when you change your primary residence?

.

Matilda,

What was a seven-year-old doing at a cocktail party?

.

Harry,

I don't know, she's privileged. Loft in Tribeca. I can't remember her name, but she's going to be very angry if she doesn't get Samantha.

.

Matilda,

Maybe Mom has a point.

.

Harry,

Don't defend her behavior again.

.

Hey Matilda,

You OK? You seem a little on edge.

.

Dear Harry,

I would rather laugh with the sinners than cry with the saints.

.

Matilda,

I'm going to need more to go on.

.

Harry,

OK, I'm just going to tell you. I must lance that boil, as you so indelicately put it. Disgusting, Harry.

I'll make it like a story: Here is something that has happened to my "friend." She is in quite the pickle.

Jane Doe was a nice person. She really believed this. She was not troubled, she came from a relatively good home, she was loved. (She did go to a subpar public high school, with many opportunities for bad influences, but came out relatively unscathed.) She went to an Ivy League college, which was the one and only thing she did that ever impressed her grandmother. She made friends with the artsy kids. She was just angsty enough to be interesting, but not enough to be perplexing to adults (except the grandmother).

She moved to New York City after college with the rest of the artsy folks, and settled in. Perhaps she's a production assistant at a magazine. Maybe she finds that unfulfilling and takes out loans and enrolls in art school. It's hard. Perhaps she starts to doubt her innate belief in herself during that time, as she stands in front of her pictures, defending them feebly. She dates a few people and likes them too quickly and then feels overly committed and bolts. She becomes really good at wine tasting in quantity, because it brings her joy and relief. Also tequila.

She starts being interested too quickly in a younger friend of a friend who slays her with the line "You're like the female version of myself." She finds this charming, but much later will realize it's maybe rather self-centered. Jane Doe's art isn't going so well at this time. She's been spending a lot of time by herself. One night she spies her crush in a bar and has some extra tequila for strength. The crush isn't very interested in her, it seems. But they start talking.

She's speaking about herself, her life, embellishing some details in a normal way. But then, out of nowhere, like a lightning bolt, this sentence occurs to her to say:

"You know, I had a twin who died. I think about him a lot."

This was a strange statement to make, as Jane did in fact have a twin, a brother. But he was very much alive. Perhaps he was a professor at a state school in Connecticut. Perhaps they were very close.

As soon as she uttered this made-up lie, Jane realized she had entered uncomfortable territory and started to rescind it. "Just kidding!" she was sure she was about to exclaim, and order them another round as an apology for her silliness.

But the crush spoke first, leaning in, eyes wide, bright with something like excitement, with new interest in her, an extreme intensity.

"I had a twin who died, too! That's crazy! What are the odds?! He had leukemia. We were ten."

And then she was stuck.

And REALLY. Was this all her fault? Because what WERE the odds???

Jane moved in with the crush soon after this incident, their bond strengthened by their mutual truths, which they had never told anyone else in the city. They spoke about their twins often. It was why he loved her, and the only reason they had a real future together.

Jane was very very anxious about this.

THE END.

.

Hey Matilda,

So I take it you're Jane Doe. This is pretty intense, even for you.

.

Harry,

I know. Jane's been practicing a lot of deep breathing and self-medicating. It's been almost a year since that night and the situation is becoming a touch suffocating. I don't know how to help her. Do you have any ideas?

.

Matilda,

Aren't you bringing this guy home for the holidays? This is going to be a shit show. Why would you say I had *died*? That's really super disturbing, Matilda.

·

Harry,

You'll act as my cousin who is very close to the family! It will be OK, he won't need to know.

I don't know *why* I said it, Harry.

Don't things ever just come out of your mouth like a surprise? Like you're writing the novel of your life *as you live it*—narrating the present, as you just told me to do?!

·

Matilda,

I save the fiction for my fiction, Matilda. Don't twist my words.

·

Harry,

I'm sorry, I made a mistake. I told you I was worried about telling you. But you don't have to take it so *personally*.

·

Matilda,

What if this relationship doesn't end as I predicted? You're going to keep my existence a secret forever?

·

Harry,

We'll cross that bridge when we come to it.

.

Matilda,

You will cross that bridge. You can leave me out of your games.

.

Harry,

There was a tub of holiday popcorn in the dentist's waiting area
today. What is wrong with people, they just WANT you to fail?
Caramel, Harry!

.

Matilda,

I'm not in the mood.

Here's the deal: You either need to tell your boyfriend the truth, or
break up with him. Either way, you should go back to therapy. I feel
like you've sort of upped the ante here. This can't conceivably end
well with him, aside from my own irritation.

.

Harry,

Therapy continues to cost money. I'm OK. I can never tell
him. And who breaks up with someone they have a dead

twin connection with?? Don't be crazy. I'd rather convince everyone ELSE I have a twin who died. Maybe we were triplets?

.

Matilda,

No. Just suck it up and admit what you did.

.

Harry,

I feel like there's a way to avoid that particular path.

.

Matilda,

You're physically unable to admit fault. Your father's child.

.

Harry,

That's not true! I feel faulty all the time!

I mean, am I even a good person? Often my first instinct is not the moral or ethical choice, and very often I go through with it. I once stole lip gloss from my best friend, Harry—and then COVERED IT UP. I was twelve. Maybe I'm bad to the core.

I think I should make a list.

Harry,

I'm always in flux! Always learning new things! Three honey turkeys on rye with aioli and a tuna melt (Gruyère and capers).

Delicious.

.

Matilda,

I'll make a beet Reuben. Beets are all the rage out here in the sticks.

.

Harry,

I said make something delicious, not a snack that tastes of dirt.

.

Matilda,

Perhaps you should take a multivitamin. Vegetables help us keep our brains and minds happy, you know.

.

Harry,

Time magazine's 30 under 30 issue came out today. So today shall henceforth be known as Drinking Day.

Three younger people from college are on the list.

Matilda,

See my previous message. Also, imbibing alcohol during daylight can't be good.

·

Harry,

Maybe it would be good for you, Harry, doing something wildly inappropriate like day-drinking. The last time you did something truly naughty was when you went for a month eating Froot Loops every night for dinner while Mom was having divorce distraction. And you only did that because I dared you.

Without me you'd be a hopeless priss.

·

Matilda,

I think I just might surprise you someday. Anyway, I find anxiety an unfortunate distraction. Because—as you are so quick to point out—we'll all be dead soon enough.

·

Harry,

I wonder if my life would feel empty without anxiety, like a central character from my life was suddenly absent.

Like there'd been a death.

Hey Harry,

I'm back from that wedding upstate. Not a bad one, though it initially took me a while to find the bride. They keep them in a room, you know, before the ceremony. I call it the holding pen. The bride hangs in there before it's time for her to approach the gangplank.

It was at the end of a long hallway that smelled palpably of brown paint. It reminded me of the time they remodeled the high school with the spoiled varnish. (It made us so dizzy we couldn't read Middle English properly for weeks.)

As I approached the bride, my hands and feet started to tingle, like I was about to encounter the Dalai Lama. The allure of a bride is not to be discounted, especially in the off-season when you only see them periodically. They put you in that dress and suddenly everyone wants to touch and see, like a blond redhead in Japan before airplanes.

The bride (Caroline) was birdlike, brunette. She had a tiny veil.

I was only in the room maybe five minutes when I noticed something on the periphery of my vision. Something annoying, like a blackfly that dips at you repeatedly while you're trying to enjoy the lake.

I ignored it until I just couldn't stand it anymore and turned to see a tween on a stripper pole in the middle of the room. (The room was a former dance hall run by nuns, you see. They needed poles for their lessons.) The girl was age twelve, max. Turns out she's Sydney, sister of the bride. Sydney was dressed in a little girl's dress that was so polite and boatnecked that the child's gyrations made it seem more lewd than if it had been strapless and short. Like a costume from teenage fetish porn.

"Do you want to see what I can do?" Sydney said to me, backing up slowly to the far wall, presumably gearing up for a dance finale of some sort.

"No," I said.

Sydney took a little hop and started in a dead run back toward the mirror and toward her sister. In the middle of the room, she jumped. It was wild and unruly, really, a little midair hop with a frenetic kick finish. One movement that illustrated the huge chasm between imagination and reality that embodies most calamitous childhood feats. But what caused her to crash wasn't her ineptitude but the hidden bottle of Dom she tripped over on her way down, which took one foot out from under her and sent her sprawling into the bride, who was just then seated on a stool applying her own blush.

So the thing is, Harry—she was fine (the bride). But I can't get that kid out of my head. I think she was sent to me as a sign. A warning.

Harry, was I ever like that as a child? Overtly sexual?

.

Matilda,

That is a trick question.

.

79

Hey Harry,

I saw bright orange in the fridge today, and I thought, Cheesy Poof! But no. Old yam.

Related: Orange cats are the best kind of cat.

.

Hey Matilda,

I hate cats.

.

Hey Harry,

I've got my wedding-shooting uniform down to a science. I made an illustration for you. The trick is to dress fancy enough that they don't treat you like the help, but not so fancy that you can't walk.

Pearls: Be classy like your bride.

Scarf: For flair.
Do not choose a Republican pattern
(paisley, gold stirrups).

Tailored Jacket:
Pockets for lenses, memory cards,
airplane vodka, tampons,
sewing kit.

Pants, for the love of god.
Kneel in that aisle without a show.

Sensible heels:
Camper, not Manolo.

Hey Matilda,

Guess what?

I've been parting my hair on the wrong side, all this time.

.

Hey Harry,

Did a girl tell you that?

.

Hey Matilda,

Well, while we're on the subject, there is actually someone who has caught my interest. But Mom won't like her. She's a shiksa.

.

Harry,

Tell me MORE PLEASE. Will I hate her?

PS If you marry the shiksa it will be kind of like this book I read over the weekend, where the female lead is a half-human, half-vampire hybrid. And her mother, who is a repressed prude who had one youthful indiscretion (with a vampire but she didn't know it), hates vampires even though the girl is part one. And then the girl falls in love with a full-blooded vampire, and the mom's hating him. And the girl is all, "Mom, can't you see? Everything you're saying about him, you're saying about *me*!"

Matilda,

Yes, I'm dating someone, but it's under wraps for now.

·

Harry,

Remember in like 2003 when you called me "high-strung" and I got really offended? I take it back. You were right.

I've been fibbing about all sorts of things to the boyfriend to cover up my initial lie. It's like I can see myself going to the dark side before my very eyes and there's nothing I can do to control it.

·

Matilda,

You're going to have to tell him sooner or later.

·

Harry,

I can't. It's gone on too long. I'm stuck in the purgatory of truthiness, there's nothing I can do. I can't go back, and I can't go forward. It's a mess. It's a puzzle. It's a riddle wrapped in an enigma.

·

Matilda,

You absolutely must talk to someone about this who isn't me, because I'm just going to get too angry.

.

Harry,

Heard an apropos radio piece today. On people who are truthful with themselves. Turns out those folks who are truly honest— like the swimmer who realizes "I may not be the fastest in this freestyle heat"—actually do worse in life, because they're not lying to themselves all the time. They don't win the heat, they don't win at life, and overall they're less happy.

What this tells me is I've got it BACKWARD. I'm lying to my boyfriend, but telling the truth to myself. I'm doomed.

I haven't washed my hair in a week.

.

Matilda,

I've booked you a therapy session and paid for it. I'll send you the address.

.

Harry,

Does anyone know what it is for love Meat Loaf won't do? I'd sincerely like to know.

.

Matilda,

Just break up with him. Clean start. You don't even have to tell him why.

Then get right back on the horse. Go into a cheese shop and find the cutest cheese guy at the counter and ask him out.

.

Harry,

That's like racial profiling, except for dating and with mozzarella.

.

Matilda,

Except this is entirely defensible.

.

Harry,

I'm quitting photography. I have two excellent business ideas. I'm going to be a businesswoman. Choose which one:

1. Candy corn on the cob. Put that near every checkout counter in America on October 28, and you're a multi-millionaire by Halloween.
2. A restaurant called Wedding. The waiters would be dressed like caterers, and you'd have little checklists of appetizers to order, like maki. You could order one of each

if you wanted. All the best tasty bites from weddings, like scallops wrapped in bacon and mini-hamburgers.

·

Matilda,

I choose #3. What did the therapist say?

·

Harry,

You know this therapist was our NEIGHBOR twenty years ago and knew Dad? Creepy. My takeaway was that it's remarkable that the lie I chose to tell in this situation happened to coincide with his twin truth. I mean, the therapist was seriously knocked out by the coincidence. He basically said I'm a clairvoyant.

·

Matilda,

Great. So you just charmed this guy. It's like when Dad talked his way out of rehab. Who can even *do* that?

·

Harry,

Maybe I should go to a psychic to confirm it? Look—I can prove my clairvoyance. I know who your girlfriend is. It's Vivian Remember. She of two moms, one of whom she prefers, and a bright future.

Matilda,

No comment.

.

Harry,

Yep. You were right. You're not a total priss. Watch out, though; you might not get tenure if you bang your protégée.

.

Matilda,

Let's talk about this in person. I'll see you next weekend? I'm pretending to be your cousin, right?

Does Mom know about this?

.

Harry,

Yes. She wasn't even that surprised. It was she who created me, after all.

.

Matilda,

Take responsibility for your life before it's too late.

.

Harry,

I'm afraid.

.

Matilda,

Fine. I'll take care of everything.

Part Three: December

Hey Matilda,

You can't just leave like that in the middle of the night and then go radio silent for two weeks.

.

Hey Harry,

But I did! Which proves that you can.

In any case, the holidays were a spectacular failure, I think we can all agree.

Harry, have you ever had a watershed moment where you have to choose the good version of yourself or the bad version of yourself, and they're equally appealing? Because I think what we have here is a watershed moment.

.

Matilda,

I have not.

.

Harry,

I am going to tell you a secret. For a moment, just a moment, I drove the wrong way on the highway on my way back to New York. It was surreal, like a movie, the car lights all pointing at me, moving fast, hunting me down. I was blinded.

But you know what? I wasn't scared. I didn't even feel bad. It was like I was on fire, invigorated. I just calmly pulled over and made a U-turn in the breakdown lane. The sound of cars honking at me as they sped by felt like cheers—like adulation.

I thought: This is it. I am either going to die tonight, or I have truly gone bad. Like Johnny Cash when he was lit like a fucking Christmas tree. That shit is powerful.

When I pulled up in Brooklyn, Amit was standing on the doorstep. Remember him? Our insurance friend? Freddie Mercury? He was looking for Nate, but I know he was glad he saw me first. I said something to him I shan't repeat in polite company.

We went back to his place and had RESPLENDENT relations. I was dizzy the whole time and we stayed up all night and listened to "Bohemian Rhapsody" over and over and over.

In the morning we went to a diner, where I had a grilled cheese on rye with a tomato with no red color and a sad pickle, and Amit started getting texts and was drawn further and further back into insurance or whatever and then looked at me, gravely.

"Mat, I've got to go. That was amazing, but you know. We should maybe keep our distance?"

He had crumbs and ketchup on his stubble and he was wearing jeans that fit incredibly well and he grabbed his briefcase like a grown-up and then he was gone.

And now I am going to sleep. Rent is due tomorrow and I don't have any new bride deposits.

PS After Amit and I had sex he told me he had a girlfriend who died of a drug overdose and that, at the time, he was her dealer and that his heart will never be whole again.

Life, Harry. Couldn't you just cry?

.

Matilda,

Wow, this really, really scares me, thank god you're OK. Where's Nate? Mom and I have been very concerned.

.

Harry,

Oh, Nate's gone, as you might have guessed. I blew the whole damn thing up, didn't I?

.

Matilda,

And, apparently, you have now slammed the door on your relationship with a bang. The cherry on top.

Impressive! Even for you.

Harry,

And there's something to be said for that, right? If I could
see past my deep anxiety and depression I might actually feel
hopeful for the future.

Harry, write it like a movie, like you used to do.

Maybe we'll get lucky and your rendition will turn into a
stunning novella, which will win you tenure and the respect and
love of your pretentious colleagues.

I'll get you started:

CASTING
Mother: Middle-aged actress with a tasteful face-lift who's
    thankful for the role
Boyfriend: Young, naïve, entitled actor
Vera: Half hippie, half haute, fully hot
Harry: Anyone with the last name Culkin
Matilda: OUTSTANDING ACTRESS WHO RADIATES
    POTENTIAL and self-doubt
Grandma (in a surprise appearance): A Golden Girl but with
    good hair
Dog: Fuzzy garden-variety mutt, well loved, poorly groomed

·

OK, Matilda.

The moon was just shy of full the weekend they arrived, an almost
perfect circle but not quite, portending the realization of something
happening—or maybe just a near miss.

It was right after Thanksgiving, which had gone uncelebrated, allowing for an early Hanukkah gathering to appease their mother and smooth the pathway for Christmas with their father.

His sister had been distracted of late—distracted and flighty and morbid, obsessive and paranoid about diseases she did not possess. Her city wasn't good for her, though it certainly matched her current demeanor. He imagined Matilda and New York as competitive peers, egging each other on, hoping for the other to fail.

And so it was death that had brought them back together for the weekend. She had pretended that HE was dead, dead at birth for a good story, and now she was connected to her boyfriend through it, and Harry and his mother were going to be complicit.

Harry was there waiting for her, distracted himself with tenure, not to mention a fridge full of cilantro he was trying to keep fresh (omelettes). *Side note: cooking a lot as of late.* But still he wanted to help, and help involved the retelling of a lie that could only have come from a drunken mishap between narcissists, but he liked being in the service of others.

He was a teacher by trade.

And it went fine, at first. Though he couldn't see the adoration and importance placed on an awkward manboy who was wearing what appeared to be black briefs in the hot tub behind their mother's house. Matilda held the boy's hand under the water and only glanced at Harry occasionally. Her asides were self-conscious, trying, but mostly she was quiet. He wondered if this Nate kid really knew her at all. Nate and Harry chatted a little.

"So what do you do?" Harry asked Nate. The first question ever asked among ambitious young adults.

"Oh, you know, this and that."

Harry didn't know.

They were all in there, keeping up this reasonable if meaningless conversation, when Grandma joined them suddenly, like a ghost coming out of the swirling steam, into the scene like a stealer, flanked by Mother, twenty-five years younger but miles less secure, flitting.

Grandma was strong and sure of herself and even elegant coming into the hot tub. She had a streamlined shape that belied her actual heft, only revealing itself when the water level rose to the edge of the tub, lapping over with a hiss onto the fake wood of the new deck Mother had made such a fuss to build. Her "bosom" rose up like a black shiny buoy and rested at the top of the water, seal-like.

Grandmother ate only five things:

Sesame bagels
Caffeine-free Coke
Tuna fish with mayo on Rye
Tomato juice
Roast beef

It didn't take her long to grab the reins of the conversation, which up until now had been feeble: Matilda, boyfriend, and Harry all in a row in a hot tub suited to five.

She got right to it, heaving her one-liners into the night like hard-hit baseballs over the right-field wall—with gusto.

You wouldn't believe all the teenage doctors at Hartford Hospital. A world-class hospital!

Cousin Sarah's baby girl looks so much like you, Matilda, it's uncanny. Except you were very dumpy at that age. Do you remember?

You used to be the bossy one, Harry, but now it's Matilda, I suppose. Why? No children to boss around! That's why.

She was picking on Matilda, as usual.

Matilda was palpably uncomfortable, trying to steer the conversation anywhere but near the cliff that would reveal her brother was well and fine, that Harry was not actually her cousin, and that she'd been creating a drama for herself all this time! She clutched her margarita, swirling the bits of banana that had become lodged in the ice. She shoved the home-tie-dyed bandanna back on her head, revealing a widow's peak and a small strip of flat brown roots beneath the red.

Matilda would have made as good a lawyer as an artist, since her chief concern in any conversation was winning. So while she really wanted to strike out at Grandma with a put-her-in-her-place rejoinder, she was stuck faking nice to keep her lie adrift. Perhaps she should focus on travel.

"Grandma, tell Nathan about your trips with Grandpa. About Egypt?"

"Oh, I've always wanted to go to Egypt, or Tunisia, actually. And Morocco, especially," said Nate.

"Yes, well, traveling on that scale takes quite a bit of money and planning."

"I used to travel a lot with my grandfather, actually. He was always doing research for his books."

"Oh, was he a writer?"

"Yes, you may have heard of him; his name was Saul Bellow."

"Oh, well! Of course I have!" The seal shape played excitedly on the water, and Matilda smiled just a little. So HERE was the golden egg about the boyfriend.

"SAUL BELLOW! WHY DIDN'T YOU SAY SO!" Mother came out of the shadows, holding Freddy, their old dog. Half Pekingese, half poodle, very smelly, overloved.

Harry kicked Matilda under the water, not too hard (maybe slightly harder than he meant to), and she yelped. She kicked him back, quite hard.

"You two, for siblings you're awfully aggressive, I always thought so!" scolded Grandma loudly.

Shit.

Matilda downed her drink. Harry slid into the water. Nate leaned forward.

"Wait, what?" Nate said. He turned to Matilda for a beat, pushed what flop remained of his hair out of his eyes. He looked a little steely, if such a thing were possible for him. He looked almost mean, Harry thought.

"Fuck! I'm sorry, OK! I'm not fucking perfect!" Matilda smacked her hand down on the water, splashing it up into the night. The droplets rose high, and one caught the glint of the outdoor spotlight, which was red, leftover mood lighting from high school. Freddy jumped at the light, out of Mother's arms, right into the tub.

The dog seized and sank, blond matted hair rising above him like a wounded mop, bubbling on its way down.

"Freddy!!" Mother jumped into the tub after him.

Harry dove for the dog (heroically). Nate jumped out of the tub. Grandmother perched on the edge, out of her depths now.

"Koala, koala!" screeched Matilda as she ran across the yard, a streak of red in her old swim-team Speedo and her dyed hair, heading for the woods. Only Harry understood this, of course, as "koala" was a code word between them and was to be used only in a true emergency scenario. It had never been used before.

Freddy was beyond saving: HEART ATTACK, said the emergency vet.

.

Hey Matilda,

There you go.

My rendition for you. Not a boring holiday weekend, for sure. Please try not to take it terribly hard. Freddy was old and you were not going to marry Nate in the end anyway; let us be honest.

.

Harry,

A touch self-congratulatory ("service of others"!), but otherwise you're a reliable narrator.

I am drinking a Bloody Mary through a straw right now, extra horseradish. I'm sitting by my window, willing the woman with the pubic hair from 1974 to walk by again, but she's a no-show. She must be in her kitchen with Lars, who has fantastic man pubic hair and is from an unnamed Scandinavian country and has once eaten reindeer. Which delights her! Tonight is a spectacular crescent moon, Harry. The moon controls the freaking tides, Harry. That's more incredible than the goddamned post office. If the moon controls the tides, can you imagine what it's doing to our brains this very second? The astrologists are all completely right.

The astronomers, I don't know what *they're* doing. I'm still upset about Pluto.

Harry, did you know the sound of the cosmos is essentially a rain forest of chirping birds? That's what it sounds like, with the ghosts of asteroids and space trash pinging all about, bouncing off the atmosphere.

.

Matilda,

Did you know that physicists on the whole are very religious? That gives me comfort.

.

Harry,

Yes, that's a nice thing.

.

Matilda,

You know who else is very religious? Mom. Call her.

.

She's not religious, Harry, she's *spiritual.*

.

Matilda,

Either way, she's confused and concerned.

.

Harry,

She's not worried about me. She's worried about why her perfect parenting resulted in such an off-kilter daughter.

Harry—do you remember at camp, how we had the big trivia bowl between the boys' camp and the girls' camp? The best part of it was when they gave you a clue and you had to make little rhymes for the answers. They were called stinky pinkies. Anyway, I made some for this particular situation.

Stink pink:
Hot dog

Stinky pinkie:
Guppy puppy

Stinkety pinkety:
Deadity Freddity

Matilda,

I noticed Freddy's smell as he sank to the bottom of the tub. It's true, after all, how time slows down at such moments. God, that dog is disgusting, I thought, even as he was dying. I feel really bad about that now.

.

Harry,

Well, he was disgusting, *and* well loved. You can be both things at once.

At the trivia bowl between the boys' and girls' camps, I was onstage killing it with the stinky pinkies in the outfit my best friend Alexis Loreda had styled for me (Grateful Dead shirt and purple reflective round sunglasses), while Alexis, who was from Miami where she had a best friend named Colt, gave a hand job to a boy under the floorboards. Apparently she just thwapped away as a hundred pairs of white Keds excitedly rumbled the floor above her.

Announcer: "For the win: stink pink of . . . *a happy boy!*"

Young Matilda: "Glad lad!!!"

Applause applause, stomp stomp stomp.

Alexis was always so much more advanced than me. Her father was the ambassador to Bolivia! I mean, come on. How can you even compete with someone like that? She was a willowy five feet nine inches by fifth grade, her hair down her back in self-woven shiny French braids. She had a working knowledge of all the Latin roots, and a Saks wardrobe bought for her by a trilingual nanny who was, herself, more sophisticated than I could ever hope to be.

I knew it at the time—the smartest thing was to become her sidecar, her confidante. We were editors together on the camp yearbook. Every summer there was a new theme. Ours was: WEDDING.

We can't all be born to ambassadors, but we can adore their daughters. And we can learn the dress code.

It took three more years until I finally knew what a hand job was, Harry, do you remember?

ACCEPTABLE SHOES AT SUMMER CAMP

1. Bluchers (L.L. Bean moccasins with the laces done in little knots)
2. K-Swiss
3. White Keds. Leather, not canvas. The Wonder Bread of shoes.

And that's it.

·

Matilda,

You really have an outsized attachment to the past. It's so interesting;
I barely remember anything from camp at all. Also—and don't take
this the wrong way—Mom and I both think it might be good if you
take a break from the city and come stay with her for a while.

.

Harry,

You really switch alliances so quickly, Harry, I'm not even sure
what to think anymore about you! I thought you were always
on my side, and now you just want me to give up? I feel like
you don't even realize how hard I am trying. I am going to be
SOMEONE, not just a professor at a midlevel state school with
ironic elbow patches, phoning it in.

I saw you in there with her, just so you know. In the Freddy-
soiled cauldron of shame, after Grandma and Nate both left—
I woke up to pee and saw you two from the window. At first
I thought you were alone, swimming under the water, and I
thought since when did Harry have such long hair, did I miss
it, was it in a ponytail all night, how uncharacteristically cool
of him.

You had the blue light on in the water just like I like it and I'm
glad the window was shut or I might have heard music, like I
LIKE IT.

I'm assuming this was Vera. She is your student, Harry. You
could be in real trouble if someone reported this.

Why didn't you come comfort me, instead of going to her?

And you *are* attached to the past. You just can't admit it. And that's worse.

.

Matilda,

I did try to come comfort you. Nate and I both tried to comfort you, actually, but you screamed "Go away" and curled up like a ball on the ground.

.

Harry,

Fuck, I totally don't remember that part. I must have blocked it out.

.

Matilda,

I rather think you *blacked* it out.

.

Harry,

So you all discussed what a terrible lying liar I am, and then Nate left? I told you my most overused emotion is shame. Here it is again, in spades.

.

Or is it Jewish literary social climbing?

.

Hey Harry,

I'll tell you why I like him. He believes in himself. He comes from something. His literati grandmother encourages me and says I could host fantastic, crème de la crème art parties in New York one day. She said I could be a "contender," a "doyenne."

His mother laughs at my stories and adds extra olives to my dirty martinis—not like ours, who thinks white Zinfandel is the only kind of wine and that you can keep the same bottle in the fridge for a month and have a prudish swig each night and that is living.

Mom, who should be the chairwoman of D.A.R.E.! Mom who is completely neglectful of all my needs until there's a whiff of substance in the air and then she turns into a goddamned bloodhound, clutching my arm, proclaiming, "But I love you!!"

Nate wants to talk about books and watch films and pay me compliments. And I really, really like it most of the time.

It's not his fault that he has dispensed with the stereotype of men as breadwinners, without picking up any additional household tasks to compensate. That's his *generation*.

He *shines,* Harry. Which is the absolute most important thing about anyone.

(Also he's a half Jew, which as we know are always the best. Just enough neuroses for an edge, but not too much. I attract half Jews like a freaking flame.)

A lot of people are half Jews who you wouldn't expect.

I should buy halfjew.com.

Anyway, don't worry about him using me. Maybe I'm using HIM.

.

Hey Matilda,

I think you most certainly are using him. It also sounds like you're hunting for a new, more fabulous family.

.

Hey Harry,

Right back at you.

And there's no trace of Nate anywhere, so don't worry about it. I got back and he'd taken the good cheese. The Taleggio and the Gouda with flavor crystals. He knew I loved that one best.

.

Hey Matilda,

How are you going to pay rent this month, if you have no new brides?

.

Hey Harry,

I have procured some parental funds. I can't bring myself to leave the apartment to earn any money myself.

Matilda,

From Dad?

.

Harry,

Yes, from Dad. Thanks for sharing my issues with him, Harry.
Super rad of you.

He's been counseling me, Harry:

Dad: "Harry tells me you're having a rough patch right now.
    Anything you want to talk about? You should call your
    mother."
Me: "Oh, COME ON!!! Can't you all just leave me alone?"
Dad: "Now don't overreact! Why don't you just call her, tell her
    about your busy life, and chat her up a bit? Let's be frank: You
    and I have argued about our different understandings about
    what courtesy and respect require concerning response to
    letters or calls. Maybe it's a generational thing, I don't know."
Me: "My life is in the shitter, Dad."
Dad: "That can't be true. What are your passions, what do you
    think about as you go about your day?"
Me: "Oh, you know—creativity, aging, birth, death, sex, booze."
Dad: "Well, that's everything worth living for, baby! Keep at it!"

I find it HIGHLY ironic that Dad is worried about Mom, when he
is the cause of her initial ruin.

.

Matilda,

According to her.

.

Harry,

You know, sleeping is like practice dying. If everyone likes to sleep so much—craves more of it—why is everyone so afraid of death?

.

Hey Matilda,

I wonder about that, too. Thanks for telling me about the sound the universe makes. Apparently when you take the Amazonian drug ayahuasca you hallucinate a similar noise, and it feels like your very being is folding into nature.

.

Hey Harry,

I've been thinking about what you said about self-sabotage. It reminded me of Leo, my first boyfriend in the city. Did you ever meet him?

Here, I wrote it like a story.

He came with me to New York after college. I picked him up in a senior Anthropology of Death seminar, when he slid me a note that said:

Go on a date with me?

And there were two boxes, SURE and MAYBE. First I picked MAYBE, because he was gay, but then I decided not to be rude, because that was bold of him and he had the *shining*.

Leo was a very talented musician who lived downtown in an apartment above a club, so there was always a bass thump going, like a heartbeat. I'd come over after work and he'd pour me a glass of schnapps and sing me show tunes on the baby grand. He was shopping a musical to some Broadway people.

Once in a while I'd put on something slinky and sort of position myself in a sprawl on top of the piano, the way I imagined a young Bernadette Peters might do.

I'd sing along as he was warming up.

If I were a rich man, yubby dibby dibby dibby dibby dibby dibby dum.

Etc.

"Yo, it's cool if you just hum that quietly, Matilda," Leo would say.

Leo had a chain wallet.

After a lot of schnapps one time Leo said to me, "Does it make you gay if you're attracted to men? Not all men, but some in particular?"

"I don't think so," I said to Leo. It was particularly hard for him to play someone in life who isn't gay, because he was a young male Canadian music savant with a chain wallet in the musical theater industry who liked fine liqueur.

Finally I went to see him one night and the apartment was pin-drop quiet, not an aria in earshot. I went to hang my coat in the closet, and Leo was already in there, holding on tightly to his leading man.

Leo and I eventually broke up when he discovered his sleep apnea and got one of those scuba masks. He said there wasn't room for me anymore on the couch.

Some people are just meant to be by themselves, and maybe I'm one of them. It doesn't mean I'm not a great person. I mean, the pope must get lonely, too.

.

Matilda,

Nope, never met that one. I never understood chain wallets. Does the chain have a function?

.

Harry,

I don't have the best history with love. I'm trying. I just fear waking up and it all being tragically too late. Thirty-five is a deadline, because the distance between thirty-five and fifty is essentially two years.

(And by the time you're forty, your career needs to be established. I remember fifty-five-year-olds who would wander into the photography center when I worked there. Starting their life as artists at that age—not good. They smelled of lavender and the suburbs.)

I should have just told them it was too late, but instead I took their money and pointed them to the color lab. Which is now of course obsolete, itself.

.

Matilda,

That is much like tenure, I'm afraid. I do understand. And thirty-two is a great age. We're in our prime.

.

Harry,

We're *peaking*, Harry. It's only downhill after the peak.

And love is *not* like tenure. Why do you even give a shit whether the dinosaurs in your department validate you? It's such a small, unimportant segment of society! You are GREAT. I SAY SO!

Seriously—ideally they are *threatened* by your brilliance and will ratify that by kicking you the hell out of there.

You need to think about this all a bit differently. What's the worst thing that could happen?

.

Matilda,

The worst thing that could happen is that I have to start over, in a completely foreign place, just because of a job. Like, Omaha. Or Cincinnati.

I don't think you understand the importance of this for me. Tenure means I can relax and work and grow into the writer I know I can be. I KNOW I can produce wonderful prose, I used to write without a moment's thought when there was nothing to lose in high school and college. But now I've lost my edge.

I just need the solid foundation of tenure to get myself going. That little push will mean everything.

But I fear my publishing record is too dismal for them to approve me. And so I'm stuck in a catch-22.

It's the uncertainty that is so difficult.

It's coloring every day for me.

.

Harry,

But I hear you. I classify all my days by color: green, yellow, red, and mean reds.

I've had thirteen mean reds this month, which is a record. I really only leave the apartment to get supplies. The worst bit is that soon enough it will be spring, and the magnolia blossoms will come out, and it will be too much beauty to bear. Isn't life heartbreaking enough without magnolia blooms once a year making our hearts explode??

.

Matilda,

I'm so sorry you're having a hard time, but I do want you to know I'm proud of you for trying to lead a big life. I just don't want you to get stuck inside fearing the proverbial blossoms in the service of making that happen. Do you know what I mean?

.

Hey Harry,

"Prose" is a gross word. Like "saliva."

.

Hey Matilda,

What's the latest with Nate? Can you at least get some closure there?

.

Harry,

Holy shit, how did you know? He literally just left my apartment. Your clairvoyant gene is finally activating, just twenty years after mine.

Nate actually scared the crap out of me—he came in with his key, ostensibly to fetch his things.

I was quite unwashed and surprised, but I recovered after jumping like three feet in the air and he reached toward me and said, "I'm ready to talk about it, baby."

WHAT!

It was like turning on the car again in the middle of a CD you were super-duper into. Something awesome, like Coltrane. You were singing out loud, not a care in the world.

Only this time when you turn it on, it just sounds like noise. He was just some *guy*. I barely felt any connection to him at all, he seemed like a stranger.

It took me twenty minutes to get him out of here.

I said that horrible line twentysomethings say at breakups, Harry. I shouldn't have, I'm far too old for it. I cringed while I did it, but it did give me secret pleasure.

"I love you, but I'm not IN love with you."

He went away.

I feel good. I feel cleansed. I feel confused. Something has changed.

·

Hey Matilda,

Wow. I think this is good news?

·

Hey Harry,

How can someone have so much power over my emotions and then have so little? It doesn't make any sense.

·

Hey Matilda,

Maybe this was more about you than about him.

.

Hey Harry,

But I *adored* him, Harry. And now I can't even trust my own mind.

Why can't things be simpler? They seem to be, for other people—Isabel Shaw from college just bought a classic five on Central Park South. Family money.

She's a child psychologist at a Bronx public school and her husband is a lawyer for the ACLU, so you can't even hate them. I fucking resent that like hell. I can never look at her again, let alone return her texts. She texts me all the time! Pathetic.

.

Matilda,

I am so glad you are moving forward.

.

Hey Harry,

Me too! Can you send me $500?

.

Hey Matilda,

Yes. But only if that's the last loan. If you need to ask again, you have to come live with Mom.

.

Harry,

Fine. Very manipulative of you, smooth. And Mom doesn't want me back after Freddy. She'd send me to her psychotherapist, who was actually IMPRESSED during my college summer of bulimia. He told me he once did a whole purging program with his hippie wife where they drank a gallon of water each morning and then vomited it up to cleanse themselves.

I was like "Um, that is VERY BAD FOR YOU, ARE YOU AN IDIOT?"

He seemed to think my eating disorder was a craze of some sort.

I said, "No, this is disorderly behavior based in my need for perfectionism, keeping up appearances, and my deep discomfort with who I am at my core."

He had no clear understanding of this at all.

He then launched into a soliloquy about how FASCINATING our family was, about what a genius, charming narcissist Dad was, and about how he could really see him as a HOLLYWOOD ACTOR.

Why couldn't Mom just send me to food rehab like all the other parents? No, I don't want to go to that therapist again.

Anyway.

How's your illicit love affair? Did she leave you for the provost yet? Or an assistant dean?

.

Matilda,

It's going fine.

.

Harry,

I have two pieces of unsolicited advice, courtesy Dad 1988:

1. Don't think, just do.
2. Drink your spit (when we were thirsty in the car on long trips).

.

Matilda,

I'm afraid I may have taken your first piece of advice. I'm rather worried about it.

.

Harry,

You've done something without thinking? Congrats!

.

Matilda,

I found a quote today you'll like:

"I am awfully greedy; I want everything from life. I want to be a woman and to be a man, to have many friends and to have loneliness, to work much and write good books, to travel and enjoy myself, to be selfish and to be unselfish . . . You see, it is difficult to get all which I want. And then when I do not succeed I get mad with anger."
—Simone de Beauvoir

Did you know that de Beauvoir and Sartre were a couple with questionable morals? Apparently she would seduce her female students and then bring them back to him, in a move they called the "trio."

.

Harry,

That's incredible! Both the quote and the "trio." How ballsy—intellectuals flaunting their questionable sexual ethics.

This seems appropriate now:

Things I Shouldn't Say Out Loud (New Addition)

Once at camp an older counselor took a shine to me. I was always very proud of that. He called me graceful. He taught basketball and photography. He was thirty and I was fifteen. I had ill-conceived hair and braces.

We held hands once. MAGIC. His hands were huge.

Maybe I was wrong about her. I mean, who am I to blow against the wind.

Harry, did you know around the Civil War PTSD used to be called nostalgia? All the soldiers came home suffering from nostalgia. Maybe that's what we have.

.

Matilda,

I found out today that all the days are named for the planets. How did we not know this already?

Monday—Moon
Tuesday—Mars
Wednesday—Mercury
Thursday—Jupiter
Friday—Venus
Saturday—Saturn
Sunday—Sun!

.

Harry,

Oh my god, that is incredible.

.

Matilda,

I'm glad Vera pointed it out.

.

Harry,

You know that moment on a bus where you pass an imaginary line and stop looking back and start looking forward? It happened to me every summer as we were shipped off to camp, somewhere around Worcester.

Anyway, I think staring down those oncoming cars was that moment for me. Or maybe when Nate came back. I feel slightly invincible. Still broke, but invincible.

·

Matilda,

I'm doing a little research on "regret" for my class this week. What would you say are your biggest regrets?

·

Harry,

Who, me? Why, what are YOUR biggest regrets? Are you regretting schtupping your student and risking the slammer yet?

Well, *Regrets, I've had a few*. I was once offered a job at a start-up in California. Let's call it Instatweet. The job came with a lot of stock options, but I decided against moving out there because it's too pleasant in California and I might discover true happiness from so much sunshine.

And then later the company went public for a record sum.

·

Matilda,

I'm really stressed out. I think my tenure might really be in danger.

.

Harry,

Well, *my luck* is really starting to turn—the universe is beginning to shift. I got a call yesterday that the wedding photographer I'm a backup for went into early labor, and I got a wedding out of thin air! A big situation at a Midtown hotel.

.

Matilda,

Wedding photographers have backup photographers?

.

Harry,

Of course! We're as important as midwives, you can't have your affair go undocumented!

.

Matilda,

I suppose that is true.

.

Hey Harry,

I hung out with my friend Anne yesterday. She came over and made me do a downward-facing dog. I did it a little drunk, though, since it was happy hour. Did you know there are a lot of people in New York who go to yoga class drunk? It's a whole thing. I would be fucking ashamed to do that.

Anne wants to break up with her boyfriend because she hates him, but first she wants to see if he'll propose so they can get married.

"Sometimes I look at men online just to envision an alternate future," she told me. "Is that wrong?"

"I do that, too! It's only natural. I mean—I look at cashmere sweaters online all the time, too, but I would never act on it. I stick with merino wool, because I know that's where I belong."

"Well, there's this doctor on there," she said. "I think he has braces because he smiles with his mouth closed, but I'm curious about him."

"Oh, yeah. The doctor with braces, I've seen him on there," I said. "He's doesn't seem very smart. And he's just a dermatologist."

"Oh, OK, you can have him, then."

"No, no, I don't want him. Although can you imagine how Grandma would react if I brought home a doctor?"

"I won't date him, I'll let you have him," said Anne.

See, that's the kind of friend Anne is. She will give you a freaking dermatologist. Maybe I'll call him up, what could it hurt? Dermatologists are the best doctors to marry because no one calls them in the middle of the night dying of itchy skin. Although that must happen sometimes, because this is New York.

Anne is starting to have sleepless, scattered thirty-five-year-old hair, but without the baby. I'm slightly concerned. Next she'll have the sensible squibble of the forty-fives. See?

Harry,

I'm going to have a great year, I can feel it.

.

Matilda,

I'm really, really happy to hear that.

.

Matilda,

Vera's being published in *The New Yorker,* except she's not. I mean, she doesn't know. I mean—we have to talk.

·

Harry,

Wow, this Vera is full of surprises! Aren't you jealous, though?

I'll call you later. Tonight I have a date with a doctor.

Part Four: January

Harry,

I'm writing the story of our life. I've got a little bit already.
Someone told me once that you start with where you come from,
so I'll do it that way. I'm having a green day today, Harry. Third
one this week—unprecedented.

Storrs, Connecticut, the home of University of Connecticut, has a
population of 10,996.

76% of the population are between the ages of eighteen and
twenty-four.

UConn boasts one of the country's premier agriculture programs.
Its barns are home to over 200 Holstein and Jersey cows. The
school owns a dairy bar, catchphrase: "Cow to cone."

Students have nicknamed the town "Snores." After Hurricane
Katrina, Storrs was named by *Slate* magazine as "America's
Best Place to Avoid Death Due to Natural Disaster." Storrs has
one of the highest rates of DUI arrests in the country. Its E. O.
Smith High School is considered excellent. Notable residents of
Storrs include the writer Wally Lamb, Weezer lead singer Rivers
Cuomo, and Peter Tork, of the Monkees. The median income in
Storrs is $76,000.

Neighboring Storrs is the town of Willimantic, median income
$30,155. Once a thriving mill town, it is kept on the National

Register of Historic Places by its now-crumbling 800 Victorian homes.

"Willimantic" is a Native American term, meaning "land of the swift running water."

The town has one of the highest unemployment rates in the state.

Servicing Willimantic is Windham High School, which has an in-school nursery in an attempt to keep its many pregnant female students from dropping out to raise children.

Harry A. Goodman grew up primarily in Storrs. Matilda Goodman grew up in Willimantic.

Harry's SAT scores were higher, but he ended up at UConn in the English honors program. Matilda went to Brown. She had less competition.

If Harry was bitter about this, he had to blame himself. It was he who insisted on living with his mother when their parents divorced, dividing the twins. Matilda was always intensely attached to her father as a child and would not budge. The kids were kept quite separate as children, perhaps because of the parents' deep enmity for one another. Their father was driven, a newly minted Hartford insurance executive, after years in nonprofits. He was a Little League coach on weekends. Harry played tennis.

Dad kept their old Victorian because he liked winning, not because he liked Willimantic. It was the best Victorian on the hill. Taupe, tasteful, masculine enough.

Matilda had a rich-girl reputation at school, as everything is relative.

She took over the whole top floor and the turret at her dad's house, which is where she and Harry would convene on the rare day their living arrangements overlapped—more common as they became teens.

Harry had Latin at his school, and Matilda dyed her hair red for the first time after her Bat Mitzvah, though her mother was mad at her father for allowing it.

Because their friends were so segmented, H&M sometimes delighted in pretending not to be related at all.

Harry and Matilda would eat sugary foods on Wednesday afternoons. Matilda had a little fridge, which she adored. Dad would often disappear for days at a time, and Mother had a touch of cancer, but everything turned out fine in the end.

·

Matilda,

Interesting, but I think it wraps up rather suddenly?

·

Harry,

What do you mean? I did have a fridge. Remember? We put that juice called MangoMango in it that eventually was discontinued. The fridge was fake-wood paneled, like station wagons in the late '70s with bucket seats in the way-way back that were for hurting bottoms on speed bumps.

·

Matilda,

I wonder what it would have been like if we were separated at birth and then reunited as complete strangers. Would we recognize each other from our very cells? Would we project some similar aura or family smell into the air?

.

Harry,

This has happened to people, and they like each other very much. There's a name for it—the Westermarck effect. Familiarity with your own family means they become sexually repellent to you, but if you never become familiar—not repellent.

Nature is always looking out for people, Harry. Trying to save them from themselves.

.

Matilda,

But humans can overcome nature if they try hard enough, don't you think? Question: If I weren't an English professor, or a writer, what could I be?

.

Harry,

Why? Considering a career change now? You'd need a slow-paced job where you can be both brainy and in charge.

1. A head librarian
2. A bread baker in your own bakery
3. An unemployed person who reads and runs a lot

Maybe *I* should be a career counselor!

.

Matilda,

Yeah, I figured my options were rather dismal.

.

Harry,

I've changed recently, myself. I've dyed my hair dark, nearly black. I'm a new person, Harry. I'm like Anjelica Huston awesome. Perhaps I've reached that age where I can imagine myself more at forty than at twenty. In this case, I must make plans to look my best. Start collecting timeless clothing in good fabrics. Develop a signature red lip.

I think it was those lights coming at me on the highway. They cleansed me, or scared away my demons, or made me brave finally.

I have a new seriousness, a new purpose, a new hairstylist. Sharon lovingly made me this dark brunette. No more boxes for me, Harry.

Why do all your hairstylists want to malign the stylist that came before? Are they just bitter by nature? Or do they all have flaws only their own kind can see?

Harry,

Either I'm hitting my stride, or I have a slow-growing tumor blocking my brain's failure area. Will the genetic test reveal this to me??

Or I could just be ovulating.

.

Harry,

Sorry! I bet you just raised your eyebrows at that last message. Because you are a man and you don't understand anything. They should hand out a manual to adolescent girls. We are COMPLEX beings with lives highly influenced and run by hormones, and no one even knows what the hell is going on. I mean, I told you about the cat-in-heat thing, but it goes much, much deeper than that.

TIMELINE OF A WOMAN'S MONTH

It took me fourteen years of bleeding to figure this out, Harry. If men had menstrual cycles, we would all live our lives to the very particulars of it. And it is rather particular.

I had to search the greatest depths of the internet to find out this information.

Basically you've got to harness the moods and hormones, and learn what you can do, when. And then you can be a mood ninja, using progesterone for good and not evil.

LIGHT SIDE OF THE MOON:

Preovulation (ESTROGEN)/inward creative "yin" time. You can write here.

Ovulation/cat in heat! Go to the bar and meet a man. Make all the artwork. Live large.

DARK SIDE OF THE MOON:

Postovulation (FUCKING PROGESTERONE)/this is your comedown from ovulating. You are sluggish and no one wants to have sex with you anymore. Don't go to the bar, don't attempt to create art. Just nap and watch documentaries.

Menstruation/Blood comes out of your vagina, which is unpleasant.

Hormones can even tell you which vocation to have:

When estrogen is in charge, be a writer.

When progesterone is in charge, be a photographer.

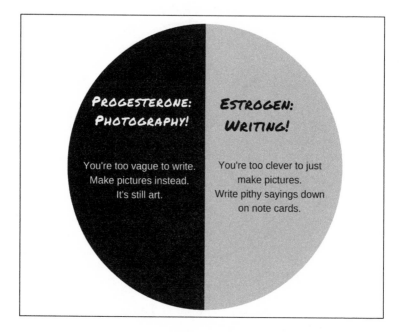

PROGESTERONE:
PHOTOGRAPHY!

You're too vague to write.
Make pictures instead.
It's still art.

ESTROGEN:
WRITING!

You're too clever to just
make pictures.
Write pithy sayings down
on note cards.

I think you're supposed to change your diet, too, and not drink at certain times, but I haven't reached that level of understanding yet.

(A steak while you're bleeding out of your vagina obviously makes sense.)

You can also track all your fertilities, but that is not relevant for me.

Being a creative person and being a hormonally sensitive female AND being an addictive personality is a triple fucking whammy.

You have to navigate carefully. I hope one day I will have a daughter and I will be able to sketch this all out for her, so she's not in the dark.

Mom once told me I was a delightful baby, full of energy. "What happened?" she said. My brain on fucking progesterone happened, Mom—thanks for the heads-up.

·

Matilda,

I don't recommend being a writer, it's awfully stressful.

·

Harry,

Is it? Because Mom seems to think you defecate gold, whereas she told me, "There's no shame in a blue-collar job"—referring to wedding photography.

·

Matilda,

That's just because she's still paying your grad school loans and resents it.

·

Harry,

Well, there are no fully paid PhDs for artists. They *want* you to be poor. It's part of the experience.

Matilda,

I don't think you should give up on being an artist quite yet.

.

Harry,

But I have a writer's mind! I have ideas all the time. I currently have a wonderful idea for a screenplay.

It's like *Fight Club,* but it's about women who resent the aching need to have children that your brain foists on you from twenty to forty. So, in order to keep the child-demanding demons at bay, they develop a hormone pill that just knocks that shit out. It cuts down their estrogen, ups their testosterone. They are more aggressive. They get promotions at work.

Everything is chemical, Harry. Everything is run by hormones. There is no free will. Don't feel sad about being babyless. Instead, rearrange your hormones. Take charge!

They should have all sorts of formulas for women—I mean, screw the birth control pill. Where is the postovulation pill? The "feel like a man today" pill, the "fuck bleeding all the time, are you fucking kidding me??" pill?

What would be a good name for such a pill? Happtiva? Vag-ex? Estro-NO-va?

.

Harry,

If you send me to voicemail one more time, I am going to lose my mind. And you truly need to rerecord your message. You cannot start with "Um, you've reached Harry Goodman?"

Yes, I have reached Harry Goodman. Or at least his inept voicemail! Why the hell are you asking me?

.

Harry,

Holy shit I just got *The New Yorker*. I thought it was Vera who was being published? But it's you, OMG CONGRATULATIONS, surprise!!!

Did you write a poem inspired by hers that you told me about? Flight or invisibility? (Obviously flight, as we discussed.)

I think I like it, I do. It sounds new for you. Tenure now should be no problem, right?

CALL ME, MOTHERFUCKER. Ima put champagne into my mouth to celebrate.

.

Harry,

Why won't you answer me? Harry, something isn't right. I couldn't place it at first, but I figured it out. Harry, this is Vera's poem? The one you told me about?

.

Matilda,

Sorry for the radio silence. The thing is: I made a really big mistake.
I continually feel that I might vomit. She hasn't seen it yet. I never
thought they'd accept it. They don't accept anything.

.

Harry,

It's true—I heard someone sent *The New Yorker* a poem that
it had ALREADY PUBLISHED a few years back, and that got
rejected, too. Not sure how you managed this! The universe is
playing a trick on you.

Holy shit! Holy shit, Harry, what are you going to do? How are
we going to fix this?! I think you might just have to tell her. Be
honest. Better to tell her than to tell the magazine, right? God,
this is bad. What about when the English department finds
out? Oh god, Harry. Harry! How the fuck did this happen?!
Fuckckkkk.

There must be a way out.

.

Matilda,

I don't know! I've been avoiding her all week, but *The New Yorker*
finally comes to the boonies in forty-eight hours. She reads it
religiously, and of course the department does, too. I think I'm
going to leave town.

.

Harry,

Normally I would tell you to face the music, but now I think
hiding might be a good idea. God, unless you can talk to her. Yes,
I think you have to talk to her. I mean, forget tenure! This could
ruin your writing career forever. This could ruin YOU.

Jesus, Harry, and I thought I was the fucked-up one, driving
into traffic and almost dying, but that was nothing. You're in a
goddamned pickle, friend. Come to me in Brooklyn. We'll dye
your hair black, too, while we hide from the law. We'll have us a
time, Harry.

Had any other professors seen the poem?

.

Matilda,

I don't think so. I have to talk to her. Fuck, Matilda, I think I love her.
What have I done?

.

Harry,

I'll fetch you in Grand Central and protect you from those
awful literary wolves and aggressive undergrads. It will be like
when we were tiny, like when I pretended you were a puppy
and called you "runt" and wrapped you in a blanket and fed you
warm milk. I could have kept you forever like that, if you'd have
let me.

.

147

Matilda,

I don't think so. I have to figure this out first. I need to stay here, or go somewhere by myself.

.

Matilda,

Remember how Dad called us jerk-offs when we were bad in the '80s?

.

Harry,

I know. No wonder Mom hated that guy. Ha-ha-ha it's funny, though. A little.

.

Matilda,

I remember feeling like "No, I'm a good guy, Dad!" I had an obsession with good guys and bad guys. And I was just so offended. But now, look—I'm a bad guy after all.

.

Harry,

Please, that is bullshit. You are the goodest person I know. You are good to a fault. It's unfortunate that your one fuckup might have lifelong consequences. But I'm sure I can think of something to get you out of this.

For now, you need to sit Vera down and have her see reason. She needs to cover your back.

.

Matilda,

She has no reason to want to do that.

.

Harry,

Sure she does. She doesn't want scandal. She doesn't want to tarnish her good name.

.

Matilda,

What do you mean? How would this tarnish *her*? This is *my career* we're talking about.

.

Harry,

You are thinking about this incorrectly. You are feeling lost and defensive. You are that guy on the message asking if you are Harry Goodman. I, however, am Anjelica fucking Huston.

You must give Vera a view of the future. Her future after she helps you in this unfortunate slip up? Or her future after she throws you to the wolves? It is her choice, her fork in the road.

She thinks you're swell, and she likes lobsters, so there must be true wisdom deep in her sophisticated four-name hippie heart.

.

Matilda,

You mean threaten her? I love her! I've done something terrible to her! I would never forgive me if I were in her position, and now I threaten her to cover my fuckup? It doesn't make any sense. And what leverage do I even have? I give her a bad grade? Jesus. She could tell them anything. Matilda, we're sleeping together.

.

Harry,

Oh, Harry! I'm so shocked! Tell me another!

.

Harry,

Calm, please. Ice water in veins, please. We have forty-four hours until shit on fan. Something will come to light.

BTW, I just read an excellent piece about artists and creating in *The New York Times*:

> *In the popular imagination, artists tend to exist either at the pinnacle of fame and luxury or in the depths of penury and obscurity—rarely in the middle, where most of the rest of us toil and dream. They are subject to admiration, envy, resentment and contempt, but it is odd how seldom their efforts are understood as work.*

Harry, I think troubled times like these are what we should embrace: *envy, resentment, contempt.* These are our *lot.* Let us use this in our favor. Remember, Vera is an artist, too. She has dreams, too. I'm sure she has great big dreams, in fact. Perhaps you've discussed them with her?

.

Matilda,

I don't know.

.

Harry,

Please have more testicles. Do not be the twelve-year-old boy who votes for his opponent for student council.

You're not going down this easy, and certainly not because of her.

.

Harry,

Things sometimes appear differently in our minds than they do in actuality. Take, for example, the jackalope. Lore had it that these mythical creatures were a fantastical cross between a jack rabbit and an antelope. But, in fact, they were simply BUNNIES WITH CANCER. They had tumors spurred by the *Shope papilloma* virus, which causes horn- and antlerlike growths on the head.

So not magical, just sad.

Here's a visual. This bunny has cancer.

.

Matilda,

What are you talking about?

.

Harry,

We are all primarily spiritual beings; we are just having a
temporary physical experience. A French philosopher said that.

.

Matilda,

Please stop. I'm not in the mood to try to follow you.

.

Harry,

When all is well and you are a famous writer in ten years, you must start using your full name. Harrison Angus Goodman. Writers have three names if they're any good. If you fail at writing and become a lawyer, you may use just the middle initial. Harry A. Goodman. If you fail the bar and are forced to become a pop star, you may simple go by: Harrison.

·

Matilda,

Enough.

·

Harry,

Just giving you some options.

TTYL8r.

·

Matilda,

I can barely sleep next to Vera at night. I feel like I'm living a complete lie. I wake up in a panic, my heart beating through my chest, and I swear she must be able to hear its beating, to smell my lie, my very ungoodness. I can't stand this feeling, Matilda! I feel like I am losing my mind.

·

Harry,

Huh. I feel that way all the time. Once a month, in fact. Maybe that's why men are less good at emotions—women are literally trained by being hormonally whiplashed all fucking month long.

.

Matilda,

I have to talk to her soon. And I have a voicemail on my phone from the head of the English department, congratulating me. I think the new issue is out online. Vera's going to see it any minute.

"What a delightful surprise, Mr. Goodman! I would have thought you'd have informed us of this accomplishment weeks ago. Looking forward to discussing your future in the department! Unless you're too big for us now, ha-ha-ha."

Oh god. This guy just wants to bury me. When he finds out the truth he is going to be absolutely pumped. I once heard him talking about me at an interdepartmental cocktail party with the philosophers after too many whiskeys: "Pseudointellectual, overambitious, pretentious . . . *McSweeney's* reading, something something." It couldn't have been positive.

.

Harry,

I think you need to channel brave, baller (word we should use more), future Harry. Imagine exactly who you want to be in ten years—head of the department yourself, perhaps? Routinely featured in *The New Yorker*? On a book tour? And speak to Vera as that person.

You need to do this today, Harry. You need to own the situation.
I've seen this on TV. You write the story before they write it.

·

Matilda,

OK, I'm going to talk to Vera today. I'm going to take a beta-
blocker and go for a run and then pull her aside after class. At least
then I will still have the air of authority on me, if I have any left. She
always seems most affectionate right after class.

·

Harry,

Do it. Do it now. Believe me—this part here, this is the hardest
part. The waiting.

Wow! Maybe that's why I had a plane crash dream last night—to
relay that message to you.

I think the dream was symbolic of the scariest thing to me—
knowing that you're going to die, and knowing When, and then
having to wait for it. The waiting is always the hardest part. I
can't tell you how many waiting rooms/vestibules/coffee shops
I've had to pop Xanaxes in.

(Dying in a plane probably isn't the worst way to go. You have a
hell of a ride, you pass out, you disintegrate on impact. But gin
would definitely help. Dad had some Ativan with him, too—he
was on the plane with me, god bless him. Ativan always just
makes me sleepy.)

Hierarchy of antipanic drugs, best to worst:

KLONOPIN—blue ribbon
XANAX—red ribbon
ATIVAN—yellow ribbon

Don't you find ribbons and their corresponding colors fascinating? How did they decide blue is best?

Anyway! Go talk to her, Harry. Just tell her what you did, and that you are so sorry.

Actually, WAIT—maybe the dream was meant to convey the good news that AT LEAST YOU'RE NOT DYING! What's the worst thing that could happen here?

.

Matilda,

I could lose my job, my career, my good name, and my girlfriend. I mean, fuck tenure.

.

Harry,

Talking Points

You sent the poem in during a fit of insanity (her poem was so brilliant!) and didn't imagine they'd ever take it. Tell her you will make it up to her, and that it is important that she not ruin your career over this. It is important for both of your careers, in fact.

Stress that if she goes to the head of the department, your relationship will come to light, and you will both be quite embarrassed. She will likely have to leave the university as a student. The scandal might light up the internet. The intellectual elite will cream its jeans over a college professor stealing a student's work and getting it into *The New Yorker*. CREAM ITS JEANS.

Do this now and then I will give you further instructions.

DO it. Waiting is the hardest part.

.

Mat,

Fuck.

.

Harry,

I am sending you brave thoughts right now. Just like when 10,000 people send healing thoughts to a child with cancer and the child recovers.

.

Harry,

Still thinking of you. I have my prayer beads out, the ones I got in Greece when I went there to build a road for a poor town during the summer with thirteen fellow upper-middle-class youths who just wanted to give each other hand jobs under blankets in tour buses outside the Parthenon while high on ouzo.

I believe we built a road to nowhere solely to satisfy our parents' do-gooder requirement that justified sending us on such a trip;

I remember looking at this fifty-yard cement runway that led from the outskirts of town down to the river and thinking it was entirely useless to anyone. It took us six weeks to build.

The Gypsies lived in a kind of tent city down by the river. I didn't really understand that "Gypsy" was a real thing; Mom let me be a gypsy with a crystal ball three Halloweens in row, which may have been accidentally quite racist.

Speaking of racist, the GREEKS! Holy shit. On the other side of the river was a small cohort of Albanian folks, apparently quite off their luck. Boy, do the Greeks not like Albanians. They were 100% open with their anti-Albanian vitriol. It was the worst kind of slur, to be called an Albanian. The townspeople were very clear with all their preferences. They deemed me and a horsey girl named Georgia the prettiest girls on the trip. I felt very proud and cocky about it.

Georgia and I were regularly given the best seats at town dinners. Extra ouzo.

There was also a black kid on the trip. His name was Thomas. He was very handsome, with amazing green eyes. Two weeks in we find out he goes to the toniest school in England. OK, so he's rich. Two weeks after that, he has too much ouzo and spills that he's the son of the leader of a prominent African nation. This dude was basically a real prince.

But the thing is, Greek people (the ones in this town, to be fair— who knows, it could have been Greek rednecks I was surrounded by, but I feel comfortable generalizing) really don't like black people. Thomas had to move houses four times that summer, because he was being threatened during home stays. He ended up with sort of an unofficial bodyguard, who I think may have been Albanian, which didn't help matters.

Thomas continued to chug ouzo. One night he had too much and professed his love for me! I was very flattered. He then cried and said he was so embarrassed when his father arrived for eighth-grade graduation in a Hummer with armed guards. He was really drunk. Like really, really serious-alcohol-poisoning zombie drunk. The next morning he was due at the consulate because he had lost his visa and we were leaving in a day. He was so drunk still by his 11 a.m. appointment that he was detained in the country for his own safety and didn't go to the airport with us. I never heard from him again.

Anyway. Hope things are going well with your chat. I'm sure the prayer beads will help.

.

Matilda,

Hi. It's done. I'm incredibly enervated, but I think it went OK. I don't know whether to be angry with you or just give in.

.

Harry,

Wait, what?! Why are you angry? Tell me all of it.

.

Matilda,

I am so tired, I just need to lie down.

.

Harry,

In a minute, just write out what you said to her and what she said to you. Write it like a screenplay!

.

Matilda,

I didn't tape the damn conversation. Life is not a screenplay! It's real and it's messy and it's exhausting.

.

Harry,

One paragraph.

.

Matilda,

Ugh.

OK. So after class we met at our usual spot outside the cafeteria, under the Japanese maple. I had the magazine tucked under my arm, and I figured I'd just hand it to her and watch her reaction. Just get it all out there, you know? I mean, part of me thought she'd be pleased just to see the *words* in print. She's a good person, Matilda, she believes in literature, and perhaps it would make her happy that she'd brought her words to people. Maybe she could think of Harrison Goodman as a pen name maybe? Or I could change my name? Perhaps crazy but it's just a thought.

But anyway, I didn't even get there, because she's all bubbly and happy and shoves this piece of paper at me. A paper with the *Paris Review* insignia at the top.

And, essentially, it's a letter inviting her to be in their internship program this summer, provided she finishes her *sophomore year in good standing under the tutelage of Professor Goodman. We don't usually solicit sophomores, rather juniors, but you show such promise that we have made an exception.*

And THEN it says it would love to publish a poem of hers in the September edition. And then it really lays it on, like:

Paris Review *internships are a great introduction to the literary world. Past graduates have gone on to find work at a wide range of literary agencies, publishing houses, magazines, and newspapers, among blah blah blah fancy yada yada you've heard of it, it's famous. Others have gone on to enjoy successful freelance careers as editors and writers etc. etc. Internships at* Paris Review *are highly sought after and extremely competitive.*

And THEN there is a personal note at the bottom welcoming her to the *Paris Review* family, from *Editor in Chief Alexis Loreda.*

The name sounded familiar to me, Matilda, even in my sleepless state. I had déjà vu, as though we'd just been talking about her, and then I realized we HAD. Alexis from your camp stories. Alexis, the brilliant, sexually precocious Harvard-matriculating camp friend with the glamorous political family. The one who could do her own French braid and who taught you how to kiss and what to wear.

I could barely think at this point.

But Matilda, she was so HAPPY!

But I did it anyway, I pulled out the magazine and dropped to my knees and blubbered something like an incompetent, I'm not even sure what. And Vera was confused. But not angry.

She went for a walk. She's calling me this afternoon. Now I have to nap.

Let me ask you something, Matilda. Why didn't you ever pull this string for me? Why didn't you ever get MY writing in the *Paris Review,* if you'd been in touch with Alexis all along? All it took was one email?

Do you believe in *my* writing? Or is everything just a game?

I don't even know what to think anymore.

.

Harry,

You're welcome for saving your fucking life. I have a great thing going with the dermatologist, BTW, but I won't bore you with that. I'm too busy HELPING YOU AND LOVING YOU.

In any case, despite your ungrateful attitude, I am thrilled my first plan worked.

We're still quite close, Alexis and I. Haven't you ever heard that maintaining friendships is one of the most essential components of a happy life?

She is a STONE FOX, Harry. Those descriptions from our nubile escapades are probably still keeping you up late once a fortnight (or past 10 p.m., anyway).

PS She dated Clooney AND Jeter.

.

Matilda,

Please, you're far too self-congratulatory lately.

Anyway, we'll see if it worked. I feel like an absolute, pathetic marionette of a failure, which is not my ideal outcome.

.

Harry,

If it doesn't work, I do not quite know how we are going to properly implement my second plan.

.

Harry,

What's the latest?

.

Harry,

Are you talking to me?

.

Matilda,

Vera's forgiven me. But there's something else.

163

·

Harry,

What what?

·

Matilda,

She's pregnant.

·

Harry,

What incredible luck! That was my second idea!!!!

Part Five: June

Hi Harry,

I trust you've had a pleasant spring, despite the terrible beauty of the magnolia blossoms. Almost nothing interesting has happened to me since winter, believe it or not. I think temperate weather does not push us to be our best. Searing heat or freezing cold is far preferable for the neurotic, don't you think?

I saw your story in *Ploughshares* and I liked it very much. I suppose you've joined the in crowd. Publishing in *The New Yorker,* my friend—that will make you the most popular girl at the ball! I'm glad we can still depend on elite social constructs; it's comforting the internet hasn't ruined absolutely *everything.*

.

Hey Matilda,

I was wondering when I might hear from you. I have definitely been busy with writing and seeing Vera off to the city for her summer gig—it's all a lot to take in, honestly.

.

Hey Harry,

So you were just waiting for me to write? What if I called your bluff and you never heard from me again? Would you come after

167

me? What if I had early onset dementia by then and didn't even remember you?

·

Hey Matilda,

Considering how things went this winter, I felt I needed some space from your meddling.

I suppose I was gambling on the dementia thing not materializing. Are your genetic test results back? Is this still worrying you?

·

Hey Harry,

Not yet. Taking forever. And "meddling" is a strong word. I prefer "assisting."

I've actually been thinking about your impending fatherdom quite a bit—how is that gestational project progressing?

I do find it strange that there's a tiny replica of you and all your parts burrowing inside of some stranger's abdomen. Your fingers! Toes! Miniature penis?! (The famous scrotum.) God, creation is unreal. How is Vera feeling? I tried to invite her to coffee, since she's in the city, but she hasn't returned my emails, which I have to say doesn't feel the absolute *best*. I mean, we may be family someday, and I got her a *job,* whether she knows it or not. I guess I'll blame it on her youth. I'm trying not to get gossip from Alexis, but I might need to scratch the itch.

I've got brides the next five weekends in a row. It's almost too hot here to stand. Though I am trying, standing on the train platform at Union Square is a feat of strength; you have to tell your brain you're in the Arctic, unless you want to faint and fall on the tracks to die, which two people have actually done. Have you seen that platform? Too narrow for humans. It feels a bit like an adventure game. Like a gladiator game show Fox TV would run. New York, man. It had better not kill me before I kill it.

Give me some country news. Include for me some hollers and quarries. Anyone die in the quarry lately? Seems like we're due for one. I'm heading out now; hopefully no air-conditioning units will fall on my head. (It's an epidemic—no one correctly installs them these days, Jesus F. Christ, this place.)

.

Hi Matilda,

I don't have news of hollers, because I've been stuck in my office the last three weeks. Believe it or not, there's been a strange turn of events that has left me interim director of the English department. I feel solidly unprepared for this battle, and a little sheepish and guilty for the reasons I've landed here. They are two.

1. *The New Yorker*
2. An unfortunate illness that has befallen my predecessor. I have never wished ill health and ruin on anyone except this one time . . .

In any case, things are well with me. The jury is still out on tenure, however. They're enjoying watching me work for it, I think. I've been running (half marathon next month) and reading and preparing to be a father, which is still unreal but really fantastic. I will be in your neck of the woods in about ten days to see Vera, who's doing wonderfully at *Paris Review,* and who is loving Bushwick, and is handling the heat and her pregnant status on

Harry,

Really? I've barely heard from him this summer at all. That letter makes me feel a bit . . . second best. Red ribbon.

.

Matilda,

So . . . I just checked the local news (*Storrs Scribe!*), which I never do, and there's news of two undergrads drowning in the Milford Quarry. That's really weird. How did you know?

.

Harry,

Huh. I didn't. But maybe somehow I did.

I gotta say, I do often know it when things are going to happen. The morning Michael Jackson died, I woke up and said, "Something big is going to happen today." I went into work and announced it. At the time I was working at *Rolling Stone,* so you know—the right crowd for this news. I told the editor in chief in the elevator; I said, "Get ready for today!" and he looked right through me as usual, almost like he was blind or one-eyed. Like when someone appears to be talking to you, but is looking over your shoulder?

I told my editor "Big news will happen today!" and got a coffee and then two hours later, BAM!! My editor cried a little when he heard the news. I guess he actually knew Michael in the '80s or something.

There was also that time that I predicted Mom would come home with a black Cabbage Patch doll. This was unpredictable and completely random because (1) I had never asked for a black Cabbage Patch doll and (b) I was fourteen. She said she just came across it and felt I should have it.

That's a great thing about Mom—she'd get you any doll, as long as it was multicultural. I loved my Hawaiian Barbie.

How could I have known about the Cabbage Patch doll!?!? I think time is not linear, and we have therefore already experienced everything before. Sometimes there is a crack in the timeline and you feel things from before.

.

Matilda,

You were always overly fond of stuffed animals and such. You were much less cynical as a child and early teen. I'd forgotten you worked at *Rolling Stone*.

.

Harry,

I have a long and storied past. I'm like Forrest Gump, minus the war part. I have a fucking Webby, Harry, did you know that? Is it "Webby" or "Webbie"? Either way, I have one.

.

Matilda,

I have a brown belt in karate.

Harry,

I was a National Merit Scholar.

.

Matilda,

So was I.

.

Harry,

Well, I shot Meat Loaf's daughter's wedding a few weeks ago.
Soon I'm going to be the wedding photographer to the stars. The
one they all must have. But I won't bow to their demands, they
will bow to MINE! And then I will write a book about it, so you
won't be the only famous writer in the family.

.

Matilda,

Really?

.

Harry,

I know! I kept it to myself and it was torture. Except, not entirely,
as it has inspired the beginning of my wedding photography
book, which will be a compendium of charming stories and

174

illustrations—light enough to read quickly, but not without gravity. Perfect for film rights. It shall be entitled:

THE WEDDING PHOTOGRAPHER'S HANDBOOK

(Handbooks in literature are all the rage.)

There will be cheeky little swallows on the cover:

Are they doing a bird dance of love, or is one bird fleeing the other?

Meat Loaf cried at his daughter's wedding. He stood to her side at the top of the aisle in rimless glasses with a pink alstroemeria in his buttonhole, and allowed tears to stream down his face while the vows were recited. They were hippie vows. Rich hippies getting married, moneyed by her father's strange taste and proclamations about love, and what he will and won't do for it.

I was at that wedding. Standing in the back, appearing to belong, slipping grilled marigolds and peaches that resembled tiny golden nuggets off of trays that floated past, bound for the mouths of the beautiful and the vegan and the lumpy, cloying uncles that no wedding escapes.

Weddings compose much of my work life. But I'm not going to go into it yet. You don't know enough about me; you'll judge. Admit it: You hear "weddings" and you hear "vocation," and you want to make a judgment. I'll decide first what you think of me, and you can decide after that. I'm not a florist, for crying out loud.

(Meat Loaf did not tell me, when I asked, what it is he will not do for love. He just looked over my head and quietly removed a flute of rosé from the passing vintage silver platter before turning away, gentle in his reproach.)

Meat Loaf's daughter was married in the Hudson Valley.*

*The Hudson Valley is convenient to New Jersey, Connecticut, and of course New York. Its picturesque landscape delights the bride who considers herself "a simple country girl at heart."

.

Harry,

See, I'm also going to have definitions and footnotes and an index, and all sorts of fun stuff—informative things.

.

Matilda,

This could be very interesting indeed. Though make sure not to sound too bitter/defensive. And maybe use a pen name. You don't want to offend future clients.

.

Harry,

Who cares if I offend them?? I'd much rather be a novelist than a fucking wedding photographer. Do you want me to use a pen name so that you're the famous Goodman writer?

Matilda,

Hardly. How *did* you get a Webby, anyway?

.

Harry,

So funny you should ask! I just did that part.

Matilda Goodman/About Me:

*I majored in English in college, which my mother told me was
a recipe for unemployment, so I added a minor in Russian
literature. I think about that Lolita a lot, hanging about in her
socks. Even Lolita eventually got married, but apparently it
didn't suit her.*

*One night, not long after grad school, at a Broadway benefit
soiree at 86th and Park, I met a man named Mr. Aronson. We
were at the Aronsons' residence, actually. An enormous place
with overlapping Persian rugs and lots of authentic-seeming
African masks on the wall to show that they understand other
cultures. Recessed lighting.*

*Anyway, I got to talking with Mr. Aronson, and I like to think
I charmed him a little. He told me to call him Marty. I told him
his living room was the most beautiful I'd ever seen and the
most taupe.*

After a few Sondheims on the piano, Marty hired me.

Cat Photographer

Turns out the Aronsons were going out of town, and in exchange for feeding his cats, Marty gave me the keys to his apartment and allowed me to photograph his longhair long-nail kitties whom he adored.

Sometimes it seems like someone is doing you a favor, but then you play it back in your head and you're not the winner. I never did get those cats out from under the bed.

After that I became the photo editor at an online sex magazine. A literary sex magazine. Very well regarded. I even wrote a personal essay about contemporary pubic hair choices that lit up the internet and was subsequently copied by a top writer I shan't name at the New York Times Magazine *Style section.*

People do unbelievable things with their pubic hair, in case you're interested. In fact, almost no one leaves it be. And there are common euphemisms that everyone knows.

Like "Full Brazilian." That means "I have removed all of my pubic hair for extra attractiveness."

After a while the literary sex magazine lost funding and they laid most of us off, though I got to keep one of the Webbys we'd been awarded while I was there. I won it by beating the design director at beer pong on the purple pool table in the loft in SoHo with the neon sign in the window at the going-away party fueled by the vodka sponsor we'd long since lost.

·

Harry,

I used to have the most insane hangovers after those parties. I think that vodka sponsor made booze of dubious quality. I had the kind of hangover that not only ruins the following day, but the day after that, too, and destroys your emotional well-being. An "emover."

TIMELINE OF A SHITTY HANGOVER

You wake up. You think, This isn't so bad after all. I might function today.

You're incorrect.

Then:

Shame 9 a.m.
Nausea 11 a.m.
Dread 1 p.m.
Ennui 3 p.m.
Fear of future and of death 4 p.m.
Complete worthlessness 4:30 p.m.
Joyless hair of the dog 5 p.m.
Bed 8 p.m.

It might be an allegory for the entire human life cycle, now that I think about it.

.

Matilda,

I've never had a really bad hangover, except once in college when I accidentally wandered into a frat house instead of my friend's place, and I impersonated a beer-pong player all night. I have very good aim.

.

Harry,

I love games with aim. Hence photography. And archery.

.

Matilda,

And riflery.

I've been shooting at empty bottles deep in the woods behind Mom's house lately. There's something very cathartic about it.

.

Harry,

Weird, why were you at the house?

.

Matilda,

I was just checking on Mom because I don't hear from her that often. And initially she was very excited about the baby, but then recently I got a card in the mail that was signed

Hard to believe I'm old enough to be a grandmother! Hope she's good to you.
—Mom

So I was over there to just check in, you know? But she wasn't really having it.

"Do you need me to fix anything around the house, Mom? Any lightbulbs, or leaks in that faucet?"

"Oh, that's OK," she said with a wave of her hand. "Why make a fuss?"

She offered me (uncooked) eggplant and pickles for lunch.

.

Harry,

Why does Mom think garnish is food? Also—bullets have "wounding" capabilities. You ought to be careful.

.

Matilda,

Perhaps she was in a war in a past life and is still quite famished.

Don't worry about the bullets, I can handle myself.

.

Harry,

I resent mothers with eating issues. Just leave that to my generation, thanks.

.

Matilda,

I agree, it's despicable for her to have any personal troubles!

.

Harry,

Quite right, it makes me sick! And why do you have worries to shoot away? Your life is lining up like a row of shiny dominoes. You even made a big old mistake that turned in your favor and will beget you a teen bride and a *career*. I mean, you're on a roll!

.

Matilda,

What do I have to worry about? How could you ask that?

What do these dominoes mean! How do I push them over! What if it's a sad domino train that stops halfway down the row?

.

Harry,

Well, at least you have some dominoes in your life.

.

Matilda,

Mom and I did have a short chat over pickles about parenthood, and she mentioned that "you're only as happy as your unhappiest child."

Harry,

Oh good, more guilt for us. What about *your* child? I'm thinking it's a boy, you know.

Matilda,

I told you, we're not finding out the gender yet, we haven't had any ultrasounds—Vera wants a home birth, so no need for doctors yet, she says. I guess it *is* a natural process, after all.

Harry,

Your parenting choices are already skewing entitled yuppie, you ought to watch that. You'll be raising your toddler on organic grains and eschewing vaccinations before we know it. You're going to be fifty years old in a minute. You'll be the old dad with the horn-rimmed glasses and the orthotics who never had a proper hangover.

It's a boy, though. Sure as a black, well-loved Cabbage Patch doll named Maria, with a pacifier permanently stuck into her mouth, which was shaped like an O, always ready to suck.

Matilda,

Enough gazing at my life—tell me about yours. Any new romances?

Harry,

Well, Gary wanted me to go to the beach with him. Every fiber of me wanted to decline, but I did it. I set the date for the week of ovulation so I would be extra enthusiastic, and I met him in the bowels of Penn Station (aka hell, complete with Cinnabon), and we took an LIRR situation out to a beach that was too crowded with the wrong people, and we ate cherries that were hot from the plastic bag they'd suffocated in all the way out there. Those poor cherries couldn't breathe at all.

"What are you thinking about, Matilda?" he kept asking me.

He crept his hand over to my thigh as we were coming into the station. We have the body language and conversations of awkward tweens, which should be interesting and titillating but instead makes me feel gawky and a little nauseated."I don't know, what are you thinking about?"

"I'm thinking about you, of course." He yawned, leaning back and putting his arm around me.

"Well, thank you, that's nice. To be honest, I'm a little worried about these cherries, they look like they've been in a shvitz."

"What's a shvitz?"

"Oh, never mind."

"Are you OK?"

He's very concerned for my well-being.

"Yes, I'm just tired."

"Ah, me too. I was up all night in my new rotation. We're working a burn unit now, doing grafts . . ."

I sort of tuned out after that.

We were covered in sand by 11 a.m. In the rashy way, not the romantic way. I could barely make eye contact with him on the way home. He smelled like Bullfrog sunblock. Shouldn't he use organic sunscreen? He's a skin doctor after all.

There's absolutely nothing wrong with this man (aside from the braces) so there must be something wrong with me.

He adores me. I really like him a lot, though.

He doesn't *shine,* but he's *good.* You know?

.

Matilda,

Who the hell, may I ask politely, is Gary?

.

Harry,

The dermatologist! He's a real fucking person, dude. I didn't just conjure him for your amusement. Are you going to become the self-involved writer now? Too busy to remember my doctor boyfriend?

.

Matilda,

Ohhh, I see, sorry. I'll be curious to meet him sometime.

.

Harry,

Ugh.

.

Matilda,

Last night I stayed up late and wrote a humor piece.

It's Not Easy Being Green (with Envy)

Hi-Ho, Gary the Frog Here!

You may recognize my brother's famous greeting. I was actually the one who thought that up. He was resistant at first and then never thanked me when it was a hit. Typical.

Kermit and I are twins, but he came out first and was duly named Kermit Finlay Frog IV (tradition).

They let my older brother Helmut name me. I'm Gary Frog. Helmut is on a farm somewhere raising artisanal chickens in the motherland.

I'm a dead ringer for Kermie—he hates that cutesy moniker and Miss Piggy, too, garish and overeager—but am I a household name? Are we the Mary-Kate and Ashley of felt animals? No, we are not.

I'm just going to come out with it: there's a huge hush campaign among the Muppets about this.

Why the secrets? The usual reasons. Money, fear, and shame.

.

Harry,

I'm not sure about this one, Harry. What does it even mean? Are you making fun of me? I don't think you should write humor. But send it along to *Harper's,* I'm sure they'll love it. Better yet, make it a "Shouts & Murmurs." God knows they have no taste.

.

Matilda,

Ah—is humor writing your purview now? Well, this piece may be lame, but it's not making fun of you. Not everything is about you.

.

Harry,

Don't be ridiculous. You know what? Your knocked-up protégée called me today. We're having lunch. I suppose she's seen reason.

.

Matilda,

Oh good! Ira Glass called me today. We're also having lunch.

.

Harry,

Well, my lunch date has more human growth hormone than your lunch date.

.

Matilda,

You've got me there.

.

Harry,

This is all moving too fast. You'd better invest in a good pair of shoes in case Ira makes you the new David Sedaris and you go on a live radio tour of intellectual cities and you need to be onstage. Hmmm. Maybe intonation lessons would be a better investment. I think reading aloud is a skill all its own. You should practice.

I'm starting to think all this fame is a bad thing. I mean . . . maybe you were supposed to crash and burn. Maybe I wasn't supposed to save you.

.

Matilda,

You didn't really save me.

.

Harry,

I ENTIRELY FUCKING SAVED YOU.

I'm serious about the new pair of shoes. I mean, now you have to walk this walk. I'll help you.

.

Matilda,

That's OK, Vera and her moms are taking me shopping next week when I'm in the city. I set up a little reading at a bookstore downtown while I'm there. Just some stuff from the archives, but they reached out, so I thought I'd oblige.

.

Harry,

Good call, it's nice to oblige your fans here and there.

.

Matilda,

While I have your ear, can I run something by you?

I had this idea that I might give Vera a promise ring. I mean, I know it's a little premature, but I want her to know I'm serious. Anyway, I wrote this in an email to her mothers, to be polite, to state my intentions, and her mother Millicent wrote back that the "family lawyer will certainly draft something for you both to sign, if that is the path you choose."

Does that sound a little intense to you? I don't know, maybe that's normal . . . it's her daughter. I wouldn't have minded a "congratulations," to be honest.

.

Harry,

Everything about that is weird and menacing. Is Millicent where the Puritan name came from? And a fucking promise ring? Ha! Just give her a Ring Pop, why don't you? Cherry flavored.

To be fair, these women have every reason to distrust you.

THIS WAS YOUR STUDENT WHOM YOU KNOCKED UP. Get the girl a big diamond, to show your intention. Or at least a sapphire. Grandma Florence may be hoarding some jewels somewhere, if you're feeling cheap.

.

Matilda,

Grandma Florence doesn't *quite* know about the pregnancy yet. I'm going to tell her, but I just haven't figured out the right way.

.

Harry,

Ahh, how fascinating. I imagine it will be difficult to fall in her esteem. I'm sure she'd expect something like this of me, but you—never!

.

Matilda,

I'm really just waiting for the right moment.

.

Harry,

Speak truth to power, Harry. Speak truth to difficult women! I did—I called Mom a while ago, to prove to you I would.

Took me a whole bottle of rosé, but it's done. (I am so accustomed to writing "rosé" in summer emails that my left pinkie naturally just flits over to the ALT key, NBD.)

I'm glad she didn't pick up the phone, because the first thing she would have said was something overly intimate, affirmation seeking, and hurt, all at once, and I would have had to hang up immediately—like this, perhaps:

It's been so long, Matilda—tell me everything! I see on the internet that you've been very busy shooting weddings—have you been following my pictures of the garden? I know you've always loved my tulips. Do you have anything you want to say to me? I miss how we used to talk. Do you like Freddy's headstone? He loved you, you know.

I left a message.

Hey Mom,

I hope you're doing great, just wanted to check in. I'm really busy with work right now, but didn't want you to worry . . . I'm thinking of you and hope you're enjoying the nice weather. I'm excited for Harry, aren't you?! I bet you thought

I would have a family before him, right? Strange how life meanders . . .

Anyway, feel free to text me sometime, hope you're well.

Love you!

Bye.

⋅

Matilda,

Well, that seems like an improvement for you two, at least?

I want to run something by you. Vera has this "branding" idea, if you will. That we change our last names—Goodman and Parker-Hall—to both be Goodman-Hall. And the baby, too, would be a Goodman-Hall. That way we're all aligned from the outset, or something. I sort of like it, makes me feel like I belong to something.

⋅

Harry,

I'm a little concerned you're being swallowed by the cult of Vera. Why don't you, like, sleep on this for about two years? It seems extreme, and emasculating.

Remember, she may be hopped up on progesterone, but Vera is still the hunter and you are still the fox.

(Goodman-Hall sounds like a dorm at a second-rate boarding school.)

(AND YOU DO BELONG TO SOMETHING ALREADY.)

Maybe I should tell Vera to rein it in. I'm going to take her somewhere nice for lunch. Like the Algonquin.

·

Matilda,

I'm not entirely comfortable with you seeing Vera. Please do me a favor and keep it surface.

·

Harry,

Please. You know I hate it when you try to control me.

·

Matilda,

And you know I hate it when you're all domineering.

·

Harry,

That's not entirely historically accurate.

·

Matilda,

Good lord.

Matilda, could you ever see me living in New York City?

.

Harry,

No. Not least because a real New Yorker would never spell
it all out "New York City" like that. It's terribly Wyoming
of you.

Mom called me this morning. I feel all turned around, between
the two of you. It's like that Alice in Wonderland quote—"I knew
who I was this morning, but I've changed several times since
then." EXCEPT YOU ARE THE ONES WHO ARE CHANGING. I
am the fucking same.

She was kind, loving, called me "darling" twice, and offered to
come to IKEA with me, which will never happen but is quite the
gesture. I felt like we really connected. You know, I think the
biggest problem for us is that we're just too much alike. She's
interested primarily in herself, and I'm interested primarily in
myself, and thus a conflict emerges.

She wants to be connected and ask me personal questions and
worry about me to my face.

How many times can I tell her I like her bamboo tunics and her
essential oils before she believes me?

.

Matilda,

How many times can she tell you she loves you before you believe
her?

194

Harry,

If you're a special child but not a special adult, do you have half a successful life? I might end up chalking it up to that. The cult of childhood personality seems so important at the time. You were the smart one, Cousin Jack was the athlete, and I was the funny one. At least according to Grandma Florence.

Jack! I guess that's a story for a different time.

.

Matilda,

You have been special all the way through.

.

Harry,

Do you remember our childhood phone number?

.

Matilda,

Remind me.

.

Harry,

203-597-0777

Matilda,

Right. I always liked having so many sevens in a row. And the slow click sound of the rotary.

.

Harry,

We'll never have a rotary phone again, in our whole lives.

I shot a wedding in Wildwood this weekend. I've reset Sinead O'Connor's "Black Boys on Mopeds" lyrics to reflect my experience.

It is called:

White Girls in Saris

New Jersey's not the mythical land of Strip Malls and
    Factories
It's the home of brides' moms
Who put white girls in saris

And I love this bride and that's why I'm leaving
I don't want her to be aware that this
Gaucheness is scene stealing

And it was *gauche*. Holy shit. Holy garters.

.

Matilda,

"Wildwood, New Jersey," does seem like an oxymoron, but I do
remember it as rather verdant.

.

Harry,

Will you write about that summer vacation in Wildwood for
me? I fear the past is growing vaguer. Must be that degenerative
disease coming to claim me.

.

Oh Matilda, how I oblige you.

At Wildwood they were left alone in a room
With two bunks and a swishing ceiling fan
Four beds in all
With a martyr for a mother and a dad on the lam

Dawdling near the shore, disturbing
The youthful pledge they'd kept intact
The wet green leaves and the
Sshhh shhh thwap thwap of the water
Left nature's imprint on her back

The cherry cola, the slick smooth stain
Of purple lips upon her face
Four days and nights of cicadas humming
And Jersey moons
And Tanqueray
and just one mistake

Harry,

I still have a Dr Pepper lip gloss somewhere.

Matilda,

I'm feeling a bit strange this week. This town feels tiny suddenly, cloying. I keep running up into the hills to find something, but there's nothing there, just far-off puffs of smoke (BBQs?) and the faint screeches of children. I'm almost looking forward to the hum of the city.

I feel suddenly like I've just entered my life, and nothing quite fits me here anymore, like an old jacket I have to discard.

And yet, I can't get away from the fact that it's all built on this transgression, this lie about the poem. I don't know. Vera keeps talking about moving to New York permanently next year to advance her career, to converse with all the hot editors around town. Maybe I should consider it? Shake things up, push out of my comfort zone. If I don't go with her, I fear I might lose her. I've barely seen her at all this summer.

Harry,

I keep repeating in my mind "goodbye to all that." I'm not sure why. It's like I'm on a precipice of some sort, and Joan Didion is to be my spirit guide. It's like something is going to happen again. Bigger than Michael Jackson.

Matilda,

Tell me you think I'd be fine in a city.

.

Harry,

Check out the awesome email I just got from a bride:

I had some face work done (as a teen), and I have to say, I much prefer pictures of myself from the top down—which is to say: avoid my chin.

(Surprise: You thought dealing with my bipolar alcoholic brother was going to be your toughest challenge!)

I know it might sound a touch ridiculous to ask you to only take pictures from above me, if not particularly feasible, but if you could do that, say, 80% of the time, I'd be eternally grateful.

I love this. I love it when people are just HONEST about their flaws. It's just the best how weddings bring out the true human condition, you know?

Harry, I don't think you would do well in a city. Cities are aggressive, you know, and you've been soft for a long time.

Just this morning I went to CTown Supermarket. Aside from the very strange meat section (goat with no clear provenance), which would worry you greatly, there was no accountability for the shopping carts. Everyone just threw them to the side when they were done, running for the bus with bags or trying to load up a handcart on the street to truck five blocks home in eighty-eight degrees (me). No time to line up shopping carts all politely and smile at the checkout boy. Or to tip him, or get into a discussion about composting methods, or why watermelons no longer have seeds.

And it's all anonymous because there are so many people, and it's every person for herself, because everything is so hard here that poor manners are expected because we're all just trying to survive.

·

Matilda,

I always return my shopping cart, but I'm not as soft as you think I am.

·

Harry,

You are too.

·

Matilda,

You underestimate me.

·

Harry,

I have never, ever underestimated you. By "soft" I mean human; I mean sensitive and kind and personable.

Never think I underestimate you, Harry. I expect the MOST from you. Come to the city! I would love that. Get dirty, be alive in the way that paying high rent makes you alive (a fearful way), drink overpriced mojitos at an outdoor café with rats—do it now, before you're a dad with a twenty-year-old wife with major literary aspirations and a fabulous, redheaded mother-in-law.

You know, now that I'm saying this, I'd actually really like to move out of this apartment. It still has the ghost of Nate, and the yellow bodega sign feels a bit brash lately—maybe you, Vera, and I could share a place. A three-bedroom, with space for the baby.

·

Matilda,

Are you serious? I think three might be a bit of a crowd. And you're not really a fan of babies, or noise in the morning.

How did you know Vera's mom is a redhead?

·

Harry,

Heard of the internet lately? She's also a JUDGE, and from the look of her, quite a hard ass. (I do hate mornings, you're right.)

You know, I think I had Vera all wrong in my head, Harry. You need to work on your characterization skills a touch.

I'm really good with kids, Harry. Babies love me. Just the other day I made one smile on the subway by growling at it.

·

Matilda,

Did you have your lunch? Why didn't you tell me about it? You know, I think it's better if you don't come to the reading tomorrow. I just don't trust it, between you and Dad and Vera's mom Millicent, it's too much.

·

Harry,

Dad is coming? What a fucking famewhore. Fine. I have a date I was going to have to change with Gary anyway. He wants us to be serious. I need to work on looking him in the eye, but after that there's a high likelihood this could work.

Give him the middle finger for me.

·

Matilda,

I won't. But good luck with Gary.

·

Hey Harry,

Did I ever tell you what Dad gave me when I left for college? A card. You know what it had in it? A check for $1,000 and the letters **AMFYOYO**.

·

Matilda,

? I don't know what that means.

.

Harry,

Adios Motherfucker, You're on Your Own.

.

Matilda,

That must have been a joke. He adores you, you know.

.

Hey Harry,

How did it go? Did Dad say he adored me last night?

.

Harry,

A new one for you. I stayed up late to write it. (Oscar Wilde
helped me.)

I caught the tread of well-trod feet
And loitered down the moonlit street
And stopped beside the bookstore house

Inside, above the din and fray
I heard my brother read and play
"Gary the Frog" to a standing crowd

Like strange mechanical grotesques,
Making fantastic arabesques,
Millicent and Daddy clapped and bowed

I watched the brave teen mother spin
To sound of horn and violin,
Like black leaves wheeling in the wind.

Like wire-pulled automatons,
Slim silhouetted skeletons
You went sidling through the slow SoHo.

Then Daddy took you by the hand,
Vera danced a saraband;
Her laughter echoed thin and shrill.

Sometimes the mother Millicent pressed
Her wayward child to her breast
Sometimes they seemed to try to sing.

Sometimes a horrible hipster man
Came out, and smoked its cigarette
Upon the street like a live thing.

Then, turning to my doctor, I said,
"The dead are dancing with the dead,
The dust is whirling with the dust."
And off we went and tried to rest
But instead succumbed to lust.

Matilda,

You followed us?

.

Harry,

Nah. I happened to be in the neighborhood. My friend tends bar at Balthazar. Boy can she tell some stories.

.

Matilda,

Dad imparted something to me that I should pass along.

.

Harry,

What, syphilis?

.

Hey Matilda,

He's getting married again. To Marjorie.

.

Harry,

Oh! That's fucking fantastic. I'm listening to the perfect song for this, right now. It applies to every male relative in my immediate family.

You can get addicted to a certain kind of sadness
Like resignation to the end, always the end

·

Matilda,

Well, what did *I* do this time? Dad and I are not the same.

·

Harry,

Nothing. Everything. And just for the record—I would be an amazing mother.

·

Matilda,

Of course you would be. I've always thought that.

·

Harry,

You have?

·

Matilda,

Of course.

·

Harry,

So what's going to happen to me? Who is going to be my family? *Marjorie??* Watch, maybe the two of us will be hanging out ten years from now, somewhere on a sad couch in New England.

.

Matilda,

You never know. Dad seems happy this time. I'm going to try to be supportive.

.

Harry,

News item: I have a voice message from Jonathan Lethem's cousin. She's getting married and needs a photographer. I guess I'm lighting up the literary world, too. If only by proxy.

.

Matilda,

Congrats! It's the first of many. Take notes for the book, and you'll have a smash hit.

.

Oh hey Harry,

Alexis just emailed me. They're laying out the September issue of the *Paris Review,* with Vera's poem. Have you seen it?

Both of Us

They were brother and sister and they were having sex.

We talked about it behind the metallic shields that were our high school locker doors.

She was a classic outsider, but beautiful, with her fake, luminescent red hair.

He was on the tennis team, almost fey with his delicate hands and nose in a book.

I started the rumor.

You didn't believe me.

You obsessed later when you saw them brush hands in the parking lot, lingering too long by the station wagon.

I thought the romance could be a good premise for a screenplay, or maybe for an independent film director with a quirky bent.

He would be done justice by a rising star's red lips.

She would be played by an ingenue in Clairol.

We had the entire plot fleshed out.

They left for college in the fall separately

But both of us remembered them

Together

Part Five and a Half: July

Jesus, Matilda—

Well, this is just fabulous. Go ahead and tell me about the hand you had in this, because I certainly have not had this discussion with Vera.

.

Hey Harry,

It's definitely a surprise to me, too!

.

Hey Matilda,

What the hell did you say to her at lunch? This poem is a bit *enthusiastic,* if not exaggerated.

.

Harry,

I was totally charming at lunch. Did you know Vera used to run a camp for toddlers in the summer?

.

Matilda,

I did. Did you know she lived for a year in the Caribbean as a teenager?

.

Harry,

I did know that. She absolutely told me that. *Bermuda.*

.

Matilda,

That's not the Caribbean. It was the Bahamas.

.

Harry,

Right. My public school didn't do "geography."

.

Hey Matilda,

Why don't you tell me exactly what happened that day. See—we'll play your game. Write it like a scene.

.

Harry,

I can't write. I'm all progesterone this week. I could probably act it out for you in charades or draw you a picture of it. Maybe I could sing it—or Vera could. She has a very nice voice.

.

Matilda,

I really need you to help me out here.

.

Harry,

OK, OK—relax! I do enjoy this piqued interest suddenly, but this feels slightly voyeuristic. Fine. But I'll tell you now in advance: *There is no reason to be angry with me.*

So we met outside the Algonquin at 3 p.m. I got Alexis to spring her for the whole afternoon, because you just don't want to feel encumbered by a deadline when you're meeting your future sister-in-law. I was there first. Have you been to the Algonquin recently? It holds up as a pretentious writer's paradise. It now has a little side bar that has been updated with blue modern fixtures, maybe added as a direct counterpoint to the musty plush red hotel lobby you must walk through to reach it. (When you first enter the hotel you're greeted by an ancient orange cat in a basket, who gives you a discerning scowl. "You're not literary enough to belong here," he says to you and sends you back to the blue room.)

But it's not unpleasant to come into this dim, watery side bar for the less literary miscreants and be greeted by John the bartender, who is a tan man wearing a white vest and a more pleasant, welcoming expression than that cat. I arrived at two, because I had some business in Manhattan and finished early. I always think they should have a daytime hotel or maybe a holding cell for folks stuck in the city from outer boroughs in between appointments. It's probably why a lot of people just shrug and have a martini at two in the afternoon, which is just what I did.

I sat there for a while and chatted with John.

"Hot enough out there for you, miss?"

"It's ridiculous. Though I think the extreme temperatures of winter and summer bring out the best in us, don't you think? They force us to—for example—examine how we feel about sweating on a train crammed next to a hundred other heatstroked bodies, which in turn advances our understanding of the human condition, and therefore ourselves."

"Well, that's an interesting way to look at it, I suppose."

"I enjoy looking at things in interesting ways. I also like assuming Californians are weak, otherwise we'd have to face the fact that they're living a better life than we are."

"Oh, I can relate to that. I used to live in LA. I might go back, things seem a bit intense here."

"When did you get here?"

"Last month."

"Yeah, you probably should go back. It's not too late for you."

You know, Harry—the last time I was at the Algonquin it was in a winter squall with my friend Margaret. We were competing with each other for who could be more distracted and destructive in her doomed twentysomething relationship. I'm pretty sure she hit a cab driver in the face that night with her hand. So I came in a close second. She's a psychotherapist now. Guess where? Wait for it. . . .

in

. . .

. . .

Malibu.

.

Hey Matilda,

Let's get to the part with Vera, if you don't mind. (I do remember meeting that Margaret once. Boy was she nuts.)

.

Hey Harry,

You're not supposed to call women crazy anymore. It's offensive and dismissive. And she was fabulous.

.

Hey Matilda,

Don't be crazy; please continue with your story.

Hey Harry,

Very well! So I went to fetch Vera when she arrived.

I saw her coming down the sidewalk before she saw me and I immediately regretted my outfit. You know how certain people have that effect on you? It's like when you date a man who's especially short and you feel like a giantess behemoth. Even your voice feels deeper.

She was quite a bit better than I'd imagined, Harry. I actually think maybe she should just give up the literary aspirations entirely and be a patchouli-wearing-natural-mama pregnancy model. Wear prosthetics out on the town after the thing comes out. Maybe it could be her trademark, like a good pair of glasses.

Her hair has gotten quite long (it must have been up when I last saw her), but this time it was down and haphazard and spectacular—as natural as a palomino pony's tail on a mesa in Dakota. And blond, Harry—bleached almost white at the temples from the sun in a way that suggests neither stylists nor summer on a boat, but the very life force of the sun itself, glowing from within.

Her cheekbones give her a hint of something other than garden-variety Puritan blue blood. Cherokee? Amber eyes, almond. And a crimson silky tank top expertly picked from Goodwill or procured by Millicent to rest over a small, almost-too-perfect bump of what all would agree is a male baby curled up inside like a perfect volleyball, ready for a beach match, just hanging out under its red tent to get out of the sun. Cowboy boots.

Vera grasped the knob to get into the hotel as I grasped the knob to let her in and she said "Oh, hi, Matilda!" through the pane, laughing as we both pulled at the door from either side so that neither of us could get the thing open. The glass was so thick that my name actually came out "Tilda," in her coltish voice, close to "Teeelda," which made me feel reborn. Tilda Goodman. Wearing all cotton.

She finally let go and she fell into the room quickly, as I'd been pulling too hard against her. There was a blast of hot air from the street that was half flowery sunshine from Vera and half hot-dog air, an oddly alluring mixture. As the door slowly closed behind her I saw a lone magazine intern rushing across the street toward Bryant Park to catch a half hour of lunchtime sun, dodging a tourist in one of those huge spongy hands you get at baseball games (grotesque out of context) and an off-duty cab that was turning left with too much abandon. And I thought: Manhattan is for the very young and very old, but it is not so much for me.

The cat immediately changed its mind about me with Vera in the mix, and ushered us right to a table in front of a window in the main lobby. Vera led. She knew the names of the water pourer, the waiter, and the cat by the time we were seated. She does not really appear younger than us at all, Harry—aside from her glowing, lineless skin, she coded "born in the early eighties." There wasn't a hint of pregnancy bloat aside from the taut volleyball. Hooray for teen motherhood.

I won't lie to you, Harry, I felt a touch awkward at first. You know me—extroverted sometimes, but often shy at first, even when it's not this important. So though the martini was doing its job, I just wanted to *watch* her. Which felt odd, because I'd had so many questions in mind initially. I was going to introduce her to *MATILDA*. But it was quite the other way around.

She went first.

"Tilda—can I call you that? I had a friend on an adventure once named Tilda, so I'm fond of it. I'm so glad to finally meet you in person! I really do see the resemblance between you and Harry. You guys are so lucky to have each other."

"Are we? Harry can be really irritated with me sometimes."

"Oh, he loves you to pieces! Which is why I was actually a bit nervous to meet you today—it's obvious I'll have to stay on your good side, right?"

"Well, I'm not sure I have that much power. Maybe I have to stay on *your* good side."

"No, no. Harry is definitely very connected to you. He has pictures of you two all over his room, you know. I'm really interested in twins, in general. In fact—I'm babysitting twins this summer who are named Denim and Houston! I do have a hard time calling her *House*. Although who am I to talk, with my own silly name!"

"Really? Houston is a girl? People have gone mad."

"Yes! Isn't New York just ridiculous? These two have bunk beds and she's on the top bunk, so naturally there's a sign above his head that says SOHO."

"That's amazing."

"I know!"

"You know, twins used to be much more special. I originally thought Harry and I were the only pair in the world."

"It's spectacularly special, Tilda. Think of it: You were conceived in a single moment, and then curled around each other in a womb for nine months. I mean, you two are forever like this now—"

And she grabbed the napkin and drew a little yin-yang. They're not just from the '90s, Harry—still relevant.

Actually, she drew each side and I added the dots.

Vera colored in the yang side, adding one line next to each other until the whole side was black.

"Can I ask you something?" I said.

"Anything."

"What does it *feel* like? Having a human burrowing inside you? I mean, is it just wild? Is it a good feeling, like you and the baby are in on it together, or is it more like having a parasite?"

"Oh well, I actually don't feel that different day to day, you know?"

"Really? Because I'm thinking it would feel like a parasite! Maybe I'll pull a thirty-niner with a dermatologist someday and find out for myself."

"What's that?"

"It's having a baby at thirty-nine. You know. The last chance dance."

"Oh, dear, that doesn't seem ideal! But I know what you were saying before about the special thing. I used to be the only kid with two moms, but now it's all the rage. But very few folks my age have moms who started out together, and made a baby with a sperm donor. Usually it's 'My mom left my dad for a woman, so I have three parents now.' But that is not the same, at all. My moms made a choice, to begin with. It was very bold back then."

"Oh, so do you know your dad?"

"No, I know my sperm donor."

"So that's your dad."

"Nah, he's just a donor. Family's what you make it, you know what I mean? There's much more plasticity in families than people really want to believe. People should just choose who they want to be their family, and that should be the end of it."

"So you've chosen Harry, then?"

"Yes, I have."

"Can I ask why?"

"Oh, well it wasn't even so much of a choice—Harry was sent to me."

"What! Who sent him to you?"

"It's surprisingly straightforward, really! It started when I sailed down the Hudson River with a boy I barely knew."

"Why did you sail down the Hudson River?"

"Well, because I invited myself along. I'll tell you the whole story. You see: The year before I started at college I was just hanging around home for the summer. But my moms were both working all the time, so I was hanging out with friends at the local café to stave off boredom, and some of them invited me to come stay with them. Naturally, I took them up on it, as I've learned never to refuse an obvious adventure. I settled in at their communal house—I guess it was a hippie house, but the *hippest* hippies.

"One day my friend Angela told me she was milking a cow and a goat at Windy Mountain Farm and would I like to come along? So I started milking the cow and the goat with her every day, and learning how to make milk and cheese and yogurt. Milking days were always magical—incredible coincidences and synchronicity always happened on those days.

"So after the second or third milking session, we're in the backyard with our little baskets, picking blackberries, and I turn to my right, and I see a blond boy with a swoop of hair over one eye standing next to an eleven-and-a-half-foot upside-down boat on a sawhorse, and I immediately knew that he had built the boat. And I recognized that he was put there so I could see him. Like we had something to do together—have you ever had that feeling?

"So I said, 'Hello, is that your boat?' My friend Angela turned to me, knowing that I'm weaving some magic. (She has always recognized my magic and sometimes I teach her my ways so she can navigate with a little bit of it.)

"I got up and walked really close to him to ask if he built it, and he said, 'You look really familiar' and I said, 'Where are you taking that boat?' and he said, 'New York City' and I said, 'Great! I'm coming.' He looked confused and I said, 'What do I need to bring?'

"'Um, a sleeping bag?'

"It was out of his choice to say no, really. It was all predetermined. I said, 'I don't have a sleeping bag in Vermont,' and he said, 'I'll have my mom send you one!' So I said, 'When are we leaving?' And he said, 'Two weeks.'

"So I said, 'Well great—I'll leave you notes at your boat, and you can find me in two weeks.'

"(For an adventure such as this, I find that once you exchange technological information, the magic is dead.)

"A week goes by, and I get a call from my friend Sophie, who says, 'There's a love note for you on my porch.' It was a white piece of paper covered in rocks (there was strawberry jam smeared all over it) to keep it down and it said:

"Vera: Let's go sailing. signed, the boat kid.

"Inside the note it says *your beautiful* (no *e*), but that part was scratched out and there was another note that pointed to that and said *pay no attention to this*. Maybe that part was to another girl? I don't know, maybe he only had one piece of paper, since he lived on a boat.

"I told him we were going to need life jackets, and a white, red, and green light. I made a list of supplies he needed, as I had been doing some research.

"It would be a ten-day journey.

"I wrote everything down in my journal as we went. Every night we would pull the boat ashore, put it on land, and make a campsite. Then he would go and gather mushrooms when we camped.

"It was a platonic journey, but one of real love. I told him not to fall in love in with me, but I knew he would anyway—this happens a lot to me.

"I brought a list of songs to sing, and he cooked us amazing delicacies every day—salad with goat cheese and figs the first night, cinnamon buns over the fire on cold mornings.

"When you enter the lock routes on this particular river, you need to pay the lockmasters to let you through. We had no real money with us, but I knew people would welcome us, because we were doing something beautiful and pure. I brought cookies for the lockmasters, who would happily open the locks for us—as though no one had ever brought them treats before! They were completely bowled over by these cookies, which really tells you something about people in general. We'd be holding on to the ropes as the water went up and down, like whirlpools, when they let us through.

"Once on the full moon, we took a bath on the river. We lost the soap pot on the current and sadly had to let it go, but then the next morning as we were sailing downriver, it suddenly appeared next to our boat. So that's why I named my first album *Soap Pot*.

"Did Harry tell you I sing?

"One day we encountered a huge bridge near New Jersey—we were reaching the end of our trip and needed to maneuver beneath this bridge. He tried maybe fifteen times to tack us back and forth through the bridge, but he was unable to. The wind was too strong and we were close to capsizing the whole time. So I took the jib and the mainsail, which I hadn't done the whole trip, because it was just assumed he was the better sailor, as he had built the boat.

"But I got us under the bridge in one try. Which I suppose was the natural ending to the trip—it felt like it was over once I realized I was a better sailor than him. He knew it, too. The magic seal was broken.

"And right after we went under that bridge, we pulled into a dock that apparently was a private club, which was having its annual barbecue. It turned out the fellow who picked us up at the club was Bon Jovi's sound engineer, so he let me record my album at his home studio the next afternoon.

"I learned two important things from that trip: (1) I thought I couldn't do this kind of trip on my own, that I wasn't a good-enough sailor. But I was. I could have done it two years prior!

"The second and most important thing—and which answers your question—I learned from a fortune-teller in Penn Station on my way home. She told me the next boy I fell in love with I would have a love child with, so I should choose wisely.

"And I knew that would be OK, because I am strong enough to sail the Hudson River alone, and I am strong enough to be a mother.

"And a few months later I met Harry. And it just made sense that I needed to be with him."

"Wait, what happened to the boat boy who was in love with you?"

"He built me a house on an island, but I never answered his messages to go to him."

"Wow."

"And actually, one day I ran into him at a farmers' market in Burlington on a weekend away with Harry—our very first. He just looked at us, and smiled sadly, and walked away. He's still a boy, but Harry's a MAN, you know? There's nothing to be done about that."

.

Harry,

It was around then that Vera stood up next to her chair and sang me a beautiful song. It was about you. You should listen to it, she sent me the recording:

When I Saw You

When I saw you
well
I just knew
I had to had to had to have
You

Like a cold rock
Carved out of stone
I love I love I love
You

When I saw you
well
I just knew
I had to had to had to have
You

Like a cold rock
Carved out of stone

I love I love I love
You

It was just lovely. And then she went off in search of a bathroom.
Her notebook was sort of listing out of the side of her tote
bag, which itself was hanging precariously on her seat. I went
to rescue the bag, the notebook fell out, and I happened to
accidentally catch it on the way down. And then it just seemed
natural that I should read it, you know?

Denim and Houston/week 3

*We drew rainbows on the easels today . . . their drawings
are unbelievable!! I forgot to take pictures of them so I could
remember them. But I'll describe them, anyway. Denim drew
vertical, brown lines; this was his rainbow. Houston drew a curve
with 5 different colors . . . black, gray, pink. Then I pointed to
the empty space in their drawings where they could add more
colors. Denim decided to turn his rainbow into a forest and he
added a monkey. At first he said he didn't know how to draw
a monkey. I told him, "Of course you do . . . simply start with
the belly." So, he made a circle, then a tail, then 4 limbs, then
a head . . . and ta-da . . . a monkey. Then he added a banana.
The tiniest banana. Houston added grass to her empty space
and then a big purple elephant. After they left I considered
their drawings and—Denim's drawing was all straight lines,
and Houston's was all round full shapes. Which interested me
because I've learned that masculine energy is in the shape of a
straight line and feminine energy is a circle. When the two are
combined you get a spiral.*

    *Everyone has both masculine and feminine in them, perhaps.
however, it was interesting that today on one side of the easel
there were straight lines and on the other side—round.*

I was about to read the next entry when I felt hands on my shoulders and Vera whispered, right in my ear (she's kind of a close talker, Harry):

"I love that entry. The part you're reading is about gender and intimacy."

Then she slipped around the table to the stool across from me and shimmied in as close to the table as she could get and whispered to me: *"Forgive me, but I have to ask.*

"Did you experience any intimacy in childhood, Matilda? With Harry?"

"Like, closeness?"

"You know what I mean, Matilda. I can't ask Harry because he's afraid of his shadow, but I can ask you. Obviously it's not entirely my business, but I am quite curious. You know, from a sociological perspective. Or are you afraid, too?"

"I'm not afraid, Vera."

"Are you ashamed?"

"You know what, Vera? I barely know you. And what Harry and I have goes deeper than you could possibly imagine."

"I knew it!" Vera and the volleyball bounced in her seat. "Well, I think that's hot as hell. You know, I *do* like to imagine it."

And she reached over and took a swig of my drink.

"Be careful of my nephew's brain!" I said.

"No biggie," she said. "Third trimester!"

.

Hey Matilda,

Shit. Things are worse than I thought. And I'm not afraid of my shadow.

.

Hey Harry,

I know you're not, Harry. Vera is kind of a piece of work, right? I had no idea what you were up against.

(You should watch her on those martinis—it would be a bummer to have a love child with far-apart eyes.)

.

Hey Matilda,

Well, this should come as no surprise to you, after your lunch, and perhaps it shouldn't to me, but I think I'm in a little over my head here.

With tenure still an open question, and Vera in another city almost all the time (she's now actually *discouraging* me from seeing her in person. She thinks it's more cinematic and romantic, or something). We've barely even touched in months. I just feel adrift, and disconnected from anything meaningful.

I actually am at Mom's right now, because I just had to get out of my house. There's no city construct like yours to distract me here.

No yellow bodega sign, no pubic hair in the window opposite. No Mom, even. I was going to try to get her to whip up some arugula or stray beets or something for me.

There are piles of mail here. Have you heard from her lately? Dad said he sent her something but never heard back.

The weaker all of this makes me feel, the bolder Vera seems to be becoming. Remember how Mom said Dad just became stagnant once he hit forty?

Am I like Dad?

I think in your own way you examine these things about yourself much more thoroughly than I do.

I found this Chinese finger puzzle in my old desk. What was it with everything being dubbed Chinese in the '80s? Chinese checkers, Chinese jump rope . . .

I remember playing this game with you. You'd always pull as hard as you could, even though you knew it wasn't the way to win. You just couldn't help yourself. I waited, and was calm, and always won.

I wish I could be more like you right about now.

You know what, Matilda? I think I've got to make a move before it's too late. I hope it's not the wrong thing to do.

·

Harry,

Quite right. Make a move! I always say action is better than inaction, 100% agree.

I want to help you, but I have to break into your broadcast for a moment, however, for a live one of my own. I've just arrived back at my apartment—while trying to get into my goddamned place (I have *three locks; what is it doing to me, living with perceived danger like this?*), I dropped my keys into the crack of the foyer trestle, which is oddly deep because the super here is just a *sketch of incompetence,* but, anyway, nestled in there was an envelope, which I wrestled out with a tweezer, and guess what! It's my genetic results. I'd very nearly forgotten about them, amidst all this baby mama drama. Who knows how long they were hiding down there.

I'm going to open these for you in real time, Harry, like on TV at the awards ceremonies.

OK, here we go . . . looks like:

All clear for Alzheimer's and Huntington's! Thank fucking god. I'm never going to die! (Or at least I won't forget that I lived to begin with. And *then* die.)

And no heightened risks for boob cancer.

That's a relief. I feel amazing.

OK, Harry. Here's the genetic bit, which I guess we know.

FATHER: 34% Irish, 30% French, 18% English, 15% German, 2% Native American

MOTHER: 38% Irish, 25% French, 14% Italian

Wait. What the fuck? WHO THE FUCK IS MY MOTHER????

Part Six: September

Harry,

Isn't it funny, how things happen in the end? Like, when you have a big life moment and you're like "Huh, so this is how sex feels." Or "Huh, so this is thirty." Or "Huh, so this is dying." I bet dying people always think that. They're probably underwhelmed, like most things. That's how I felt on my drive out here; it wasn't even dramatic, just inevitable.

.

Matilda,

Where are you? I've been trying to get in touch with you! Why don't you call the genetics company? There must have been a mix-up in the lab. Don't panic.

I'm actually in the city. I came to see Vera, but she's being elusive. I thought you could help me—I'm remarkably inept at navigating myself around here.

.

Oh hey Harry,

I'm lying under Mom's coffee table reading your poems from high school. I've left New York for good. It's over. Too many signs at this point to ignore, and now I'm not even who I thought

Or maybe if we saw the true shape of the universe, we'd see that you actually wrote those two poems at the very same time, and the memory was only split later into two.

Maybe that's why I told Nate my twin had died at birth—because somehow in some pocket of my mind, I knew something was amiss with the story of our origin.

There's nothing in the fridge here except low-sodium soy sauce. How sad must one be to buy low-sodium soy sauce?

.

Matilda,

I'm tired of talking about the universe. It's exhausting. Are you OK? I'm sure there is an explanation for this genetic confusion. They probably sent you someone else's results.

.

Harry,

Oh, I'm great! Everything is fantastic! I have no idea who my mother is, the mother I thought was my mother is nowhere to be found, Dad is getting MARRIED. Oh! And you are abandoning me for a younger and better educated and possibly more magical person, in the city that I formerly loved but which has now forsaken me. Things are wonderful, Harry. The whole world is just a massive fucking disappointment, that's all.

.

Matilda,

Yeah, well things are pretty shitty for me, too. I'm currently in an internet café in Chinatown, where I'm emailing Vera from a kiosk like it's 1994, because my laptop won't turn on. And she won't write me back.

.

Harry,

What if there's no one for me? What if I just keep ruining every relationship I have? I'm running out of time. The lyrics in this Kanye song are for me:

Chased the good life my whole life long
Look back on my life and my life gone

Try calling Vera on the telephone? I hear that's an excellent method for reaching people.

.

Matilda,

She doesn't have a phone. Claims they're "technological babysitters."

.

Harry,

Young people are so confusing. If they only knew what life was like *before* cell phones (we were all milling around like sheep, lost in our own pathetic thoughts), they would not be so cavalier.

Mom's not currently answering *her* phone, but at least she owns one. I left her a great message she's going to love:

"WHO THE HELL IS MY REAL MOTHER???!!!" Click.

You know, I'm so turned around by this parental mystery that I even emailed Dad for clarity! He just evaded the question altogether.

Hey baby,

Seems like you're grappling with the big stuff! Good for you, this is life!

I've got some important news of my own—Marjorie and I are getting hitched!

It's a new and significant level of commitment, let's face it.

I read a fascinating study to the effect that people were more happy if they married rather than cohabitated. The idea was that by making the decision more irrevocable, people would stop the anxious weighing of pros and cons, and find happiness in what they have. The results were so striking that the main researcher married his girlfriend.

Have you ever thought about marrying, Matilda? Having a family? It's never too late, you know. If you do, I favor the wife taking the husband's name. To me, it's a powerful sign of commitment and seriousness. It's got a heavy erotic message; it's submissive. For the right couple, it binds them together, captures the emotions of the husband, and evokes in him a commensurate dedication. He loves his wife more, and is more determined to cleave, and never to leave.

Take some advice from your old dad. Love you—

Oh, and be a good girl and send Marjorie a note of congratulations.

—kiss and love to Harry and that fabulous gal! Will she become a Goodman herself?—D

.

Matilda,

You can't really ask Dad for life advice, you know that. That cleave line is rich, though.

.

Harry,

I feel so lonely. I have to use the white-noise machine here to make up for the sound of taxis and drunk people.

.

Matilda,

Dad told me once he doesn't even remember the '80s, so he's not a reliable source anyway.

.

Harry,

I found a clue. Mom's work email currently has an away message. But it's all vague, with no period at the end.

"I am away from my desk at the moment"

That's all it says. Usually she says something like *"I'm speaking at a conference with Mr. Senator Important-Pants in the District of Columbia and I will return to my desk and resume being locally important at 2 p.m. on Tuesday; in the meantime please contact my much trod-upon assistant Brandi."*

Aside: Why are assistants always Brandis? Is Brandi ever the boss?

Did you know that a disproportionate number of dentists are named Dennis?

.

Matilda,

I had actually been planning to come to the city this week for a while. Vera and I were going to look at some apartments, which is why it's even more frustrating that she won't get back to me. I'm just getting one-line emails:

So sorry, on deadline today, and then have to babysit—I'll catch up with you later!

.

Harry,

Maybe you should start stalking the prenatal yoga studios in eastern Brooklyn. I'm sure she'll pop up shortly.

You know—

I'm in a strange little time warp here. Mom must have had a party recently for some new nonprofit pet cause; there are Mylar balloons floating everywhere—mostly silver, but some rogue golds and pinks and purples. A single aqua. She took that from me, the balloon trick for parties. I wish it was still Mom teaching me things and not the other way around.

.

Matilda,

I've been taking the train back and forth between Midtown and Sheepshead Bay, just watching people get on and off. I'm reading a little, writing a little, listening to music. It's enormously meditative—the ultimate flow activity. I feel like I'm in a music video of my own life, right before the defining moment occurs. Have you ever done this?

.

Harry,

Of course I have. I lived in the city for eleven years, I'm aware of the creative power of trains. God, it's like you're a city embryo, starting from the very beginning. We could have done that together, but now it's too late. How fitting.

Hey—let's write snippets of all our ages. What was an especially good one? I'll start.

FOURTEEN

I always had a thing for Humbert Humbert—I could relate to his impropriety. I felt pretty improper myself growing up, if you must know. Perverted, even.

I wasn't like Lolita at all. I wasn't gawky and accidentally lovely or blond or waifish or feminine or sly.

I was sturdy, athletic, enthusiastic, brash. Boyish, really. They should have a genetic test for testosterone, too, Harry. I think I have too much of it. Makes me aggressive, makes me need things.

Remember how "pervert" was the worst thing you could call someone in fifth grade?

It went:

Cooties
Two-Faced
Conceited
Slut
Pervert

Top five insults of childhood.

Remember the first time, Harry? I think it was the farm, in the hay bales. I remember the day, it was filled with adrenaline and heat and dust and the smell of sweat—ours and the horses'. I have pictures, even, from that day. I was hopeful and scared next to that old gray, shabby quarter horse I thought was so handsome. He couldn't have been more elegant if he were a goddamned unicorn. I had on tall black rubber boots that were supposed to pass for leather. (Later I realized the rules of horsemanship dictated that I should have been wearing jodhpurs and short boots, but I didn't know any of the rules. The older I get, the better I am at knowing and following the rules, but I broke them all that day.)

Those boots were the only thing I had on that were mine to begin with. So it was a costume I was wearing—someone else's clothes, and someone else's horse. Playacting. We were at the Marlborough town fair, a seedy event in seedy central Connecticut, and filled with more 4-H enthusiasts and grilled American-cheese sandwiches than a town in fancy western Connecticut could ever imagine—this was no tony horse show, but it was big to me, it was major. It was my first show and it all scared me. The horses backing off of old, dirty white trucks, slipping in their nervous shits. It felt like a lot could go wrong.

Did you know American cheese has formaldehyde?

(Horse play in general seems like a bad idea—trucking these massive animals around, and then getting on top of them and going over obstacles! Who the fuck thought that up? It's much, much crazier even than skiing. And skiing is crazy.)

But I felt glamorous, amongst all that. I did.

The first class was Walk, Trot. A very rudimentary class. I was unremarkable, but I didn't screw up. The ring was filthy with sandy dust; there were potholes and rocks strewn about. I could hear my horse's hooves hitting the rocks and him almost stumbling. (Impending almost-doom, the recurring theme of my life.)

I'm not sure I enjoyed myself, I just sort of waited it out until it was over. Fully mediocre.

I got fifth, pink. Pale, petal pink, second to last. A color that did not befit me, but I was pleased.

My second and final class was an obstacle course, on horseback. Walk through orange cones, put a flag in a basket, carry a bucket from one place to another, make your horse back up over some logs on the ground, etc. This one I hadn't really prepared for at all, but how hard could it be? You didn't have to jump over anything or go faster than a walk.

Turned out my unicorn horse was really fucking terrified of buckets. As soon as I picked up that white bucket and the little bucket handle slid down against the side of his neck, he went absolutely batshit.

Full-on rodeo-style batshit. Bucking, rearing, eyes rolling back in his head, sweating, shimmying side to side. If they had had video phones back then, the video of this crazy freaking-out horse would have lit up the internet, I'm telling you. The craziest horse freak-out you can imagine, Harry. If he had freaked out any more, he would have thrown himself on the ground and died right there in front of everyone.

The whole goddamned arena was slowly turning in my direction and then was riveted, clearly alarmed, talking to one another (I could see their mouths moving), and then they started yelling something—chanting something at me, slowly, in unison.

I took a while for me to make it out, because the hubbub of almost dying on top of this crazy horse was quite distracting.

"DROP THE BUCKET!"

"DROP   THE   BUCKET!"

"DROP   THE   BUCKET!"

"DROP   THE   BUCKET!"

"DROP   THE   BUCKET!"

"DROPPPPP THEEEEEEEEE BUCKETTTTTT!!!!!"

Oh right. Drop the stupid bucket. Why didn't I think of that? So I dropped it.

But Harry, what did you notice about this story? The second class? The second class, when absolute fucking disaster struck—dangerous, life-threatening disaster struck—I was calm. I didn't fall off that fucking crazy horse. I had FUN, Harry. I held on and smiled during the bucking and the rearing and the eyes rolling back. I was proud. I was invincible. I was fucking great at riding that horse.

It was much, much better than the first class when I was just following the rules and trying to sit up straight enough.

I got last place. Sixth, just for staying on. They made a (slightly patronizing) speech about my bravery when they gave me the ribbon—bright green. Beautiful. And still my favorite color, to this day.

So you see—I'm better in rough times than in calm. I can handle my shit when it hits the fan. It's the calm times that are hard. It's the calm times when you're just sitting there waiting for something to go wrong. And something always will.

When we got back from the horse show, you and I snuck up to the hayloft with a stolen hard lemonade from the groom's fridge and watched the hazy sun set.

I don't even know whose idea it was. And it wasn't even sexual, it was more *primal* or *instinctual,* like a puzzle we were figuring out for ourselves. I remember the imprint of the hay on my back and the way you sneezed from the dust, and the way you touched me, first like a ghost, and then like you meant it.

You were proud of me, I think. For staying on that horse like a triumphant motherfucker.

Matilda,

Do you know that I have that green ribbon? It's currently my bookmark in a Proust tome, which I've never managed to finish.

.

Harry,

Really? I thought I let Dad throw everything away when I went to college. Because fuck it—time to make new memories. That was kind of stupid.

.

Matilda,

I know. I rescued the trophy box.

.

Harry,

Oh. Thank you.

.

Matilda,

You're welcome.

.

Harry,

It saddens me that the rituals of childhood go out like a light
when you come of age. Trophies! Why don't we get trophies
anymore?

We just get drinking and ennui and confusion and then a
wedding to probably the wrong person, and then we die.
I feel that the celebration of maturation must continue!
Surely if our cells are all resurrecting every seven years—surely
we become different people, with different needs a few times
over.

.

Matilda,

I'm actually sort of enjoying it here right now, despite everything,
can you believe it? I feel like things are really possible, I feel alive
with the idea of being an adult.

Last night I went out with a friend from grad school. It was raining
in the East Village and we drank White Russians and talked about
literature.

.

Harry,

You're rapidly advancing through the stages of life in the city.
You've gone from embryo to early childhood—mixing with
undergrads, drinking glorified chocolate milk.

.

Matilda,

You should work on your general tone, you know. You can be extremely dismissive.

.

Harry,

I'm in a fucking life crisis, Harry, have you noticed? And you've left me to handle it alone!

Now that we're talking about it, I would like to discuss our strongest personality traits. I'm glad you brought it up. I think mine is:

Aggressive: I go after what I want, once I know that I want it.

What do you think yours is, Harry?

.

Matilda,

Patience, I believe.

.

Harry,

I think you are way less patient than you think, knocking up your teenager and following her to the Big Apple before her twentieth birthday.

No, I think your number one trait is . . . hmm, maybe Passive—if only because, because *Passive/aggressive* is such an excellent way to describe us as twins. Ahem, HALF TWINS.

·

Matilda,

I can be aggressive, too.

·

Harry,

Mhmm. So is that the reason you're not here helping me find Mom? The reason you won't acknowledge that the news we're only half siblings is *real*? You're just being patient?

Or is it delusional? Yes, I think you are a touch self-deluded.

·

Matilda,

We have pictures of us as babies, we have documented proof we're twins. We have the same birthday. We have the same parents. I mean—what is this really about? I have my own situation here, Matilda.

·

Harry,

Pictures can be faked! Birthdays can be massaged! DNA tests don't lie! It's science, Harry. Come back home. You're needed here. Clearly Vera needs space or a foot rub, or *something,* but she doesn't seem to want it from you.

.

Matilda,

Why don't we give it a few more days? There must be legitimate explanations for the DNA mix-up, that happens on crime shows all the time. And Vera does want me.

.

Harry,

Fine. I'll just waste away in this nowhere backwater, wondering about my lineage and my future.

.

Matilda,

You know how I know she wants me? She just sent me this:

Harry,

I was reviewing the Riemann sphere today—one of my favorite magical math occurrences.

You see—when you're just hanging out in two dimensions . . . parallel lines never intersect. But if you simply make a Riemann transformation and then return to two dimensions, you have gained a whole new fact, a whole new reality, all new capabilities and options, a whole new truth . . . parallel lines never intersect AND they intersect AT THE SAME TIME!! Both facts hold true even

Riemann Sphere

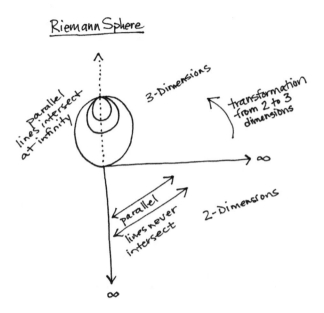

though they leave no room for the other being true at the same
time. It's all I need to know, and it gives my ability to turn whatever
I dream up into reality a solid mathematical proof for those people
unable to accept my more magical, romantic explanations of
my power. Anyone, scratch that, anything has the ability to be
anything! Nothing included.

Perhaps we only see this "reality" because the majority of people
on Planet Earth are thinking with Euclidean mind-sets, the
collective consciousness is forming the reality. What would happen
if the planet's collective consciousness was based off of non-
Euclidean geometry?!

Does that make any sense?

—VRPH

Harry,

No, it doesn't make any sense.

I want four initials like Vera.

.

Matilda,

I know she loves me still.

.

Harry,

In more important news, I drove thirty-five minutes to the nearest organic food store today. I was having yuppie-food withdrawal symptoms and was feeling very sorry for myself, right up until I found out that they make organic bologna. So you see—further proof that anything is possible.

I thought none of the folks here would have any taste for the finer things, but the crowd at Whole Foods was like *intensely* artisanal. As though they had all spent the morning making their own cucumbers. And their choices run far left (green cars and composting)—my gleaming station wagon did not deem me virtuous in any way. I think (because I was wearing clogs) I read more as a fancy lesbian, just here for the weekend. Which is interesting. Do you remember how Mom gave the speech at her college graduation, and the theme was "You Are Who You Pretend to Be"?

Maybe it also works the other way, like—you are who people see you as.

.

Matilda,

You are to people as they see you.

I'm sure Mom would be delighted that you still consider her philosophical advice.

.

Harry,

I follow lots of her advice *all the time,* which I'm sure would shock her.

You know what I noticed today, Harry?

Everyone's fucking cats are dying. I'm getting internet updates on the hour about deceased or diseased felines. I think it's because everyone got their first apartment eleven years ago and ran straight out and furnished it with a shiny new kitten.

Kittens turn into cats and die in about fifteen years.

It's interesting to realize there's an adult generation below us just now acquiring their new pets. Don't they realize their kitties are going to *die* eventually?? It's enough to drive anyone our age mad, honestly.

.

Matilda,

I have to say I have noticed the dead cat theme as well. And—
about Whole Foods—you should try not to be such a snob. Cities
don't have the lock on culture.

.

Harry,

It's trending, cat death is.

.

Matilda,

I'm starting to see what you mean about city living—in the sense
that you begin to disconnect a little, turn inward into your own little
bubble. I suppose it makes sense, when you're sharing such tight
spaces so often. So odd that on the subway you actually touch
people with your legs and arms—at rush hour bodies are pushed
up against each other almost intimately. It's something that would
be quite awkward even on a different type of train. It's all about
context, isn't it?

.

Harry,

It is all about context indeed. And circumstance.

.

Harry,

Also, everyone in NYC has a panic disorder because they are about to get priced out of their apartment. Also everyone is basically *camping for years* in temporary spaces, unless you have a trust fund. And then you have to deal with everyone hating you. Which negates the money anyway.

Impermanence + uncertainty = fear.

Are you going to stay in the city?

.

Matilda,

Unclear. By the way, Matilda—what's up with your dermatologist? Gary?

.

Harry,

Funny you ask. I think I shall bring him to the country and marry him. He'll make a perfectly fine first husband, and will be even downright cheery about paying alimony, I can tell already.

When we break up in our forties, I'll set him up with one of my friends.

He'll be gracious. He'll be grateful, even.

.

Matilda,

Come on, be serious.

.

Harry,

I am dead serious. I'm going to email him straightaway and invite him here.

.

Matilda,

Vera's gone camping for the weekend. Without me. I'm about to lose it.

.

Harry,

Well, pregnancy progesterone is a gnarly thing—it can certainly cause all kinds of abnormal behavior.

But you're dealing with an element far more volatile than even progesterone, Harry. You're dealing with a late-stage teenager, for chrissakes. You know, there's a reason car companies don't insure people under twenty-five—it's because PEOPLE'S BRAINS DON'T SOLIDIFY UNTIL THEIR MIDTWENTIES. Until then, humans often make rash decisions and are prone to changing their minds.

You know that avocado meme? It's kinda like that. Because after the brain forms you get like three still-young years and then you're old.

NOT YET
NOT YET
NOT YET
NOT YET
NOT YET

EAT ME NOW.

TOO LATE.
   —AVOCADO

.

Matilda,

I hate avocados.

.

Harry,

You know, your mention of camping brings back some memories. Now that's what I'm talking about—creating some fucking ritual. Camp does that properly. Ritual and memories.

I mean, at camp they make eight-year-olds hold hands around a roaring fire and sing "Cat's in the Cradle" to the tune of a balding hippie's guitar while separating those children from their parents for a space of TWO MONTHS at a time. Repeat that seven summers in a row.

I mean, that could be considered torture in some societies. Child abuse! I remember thinking, I am in real emotional pain here! as I looked up at the sky and missed Mom and Dad, tears streaming down my face.

But soon we were hardened. By the end of camp we were sending pieces of wood floating out onto the lake, covered in our markered wishes. Wood that we'd doused in kerosene and lit on fire, as though we were little orphaned pagans.

Let's work on fifteen, no? I have a feeling you won't oblige me with your poetry, so I'll just make a list. That was a fucking banner year, Harry. I think it's because we had been left alone in Maine to light things on fire and sing heartsick songs for seven summers in a row by that time, so fuck it.

FIFTEEN

1. At the old cemetery after the quinceañera
2. Under the Ping-Pong table in the basement with the fluorescent lighting and the sleeping bags which zipped from two into one
3. The turret, when Mom walked in and pretended not to see

Harry, these balloons are still following me around this house.

.

Matilda,

Well, see—you're not *all* alone, then.

.

Harry,

It's true, this house has a certain smell, a certain power. I feel I'm being folded into it. If Mom is not back by tomorrow I'm going searching for her, and if I don't find her I might have to take over the deed. I'm starting to like it here.

Hey Matilda,

Thanks. Any news on Mom?

.

Hey Harry,

I found a second clue today: an invitation to Dad's wedding, sitting opened on her desk. That must have stung a touch.

.

Hey Matilda,

Yikes, I wonder what possessed him to do that!

.

Hey Harry,

Insanity, most likely. That, or delusion (perhaps it's genetic).

Most common REASONS people ACT STRANGELY

1. Bad childhood
2. Brain not functioning properly (Republican MRIs show low levels in empathy area, e.g.)
3. Hungry (low blood sugar = hangry = temporary meanness)
4. Self-loathing
5. Hormones
6. Youth

I bet Dad is 1 and 4.

In Vera's case—5 and 6.

Mom is clearly 3.

.

Matilda,

God, that sounds about right.

You know what I read today? That our daydreams of the future (which are generally quite rosy) are actually "memories" we make of the future, and they are, by definition, somewhat delusional.

.

Harry,

I feel I must counter that; I do think time exists on a different plane than we realize, and therefore our "memories of the future" actually shape our "knowledge of today."

I need a working memory of the future, Harry. And maybe it's Gary shaped. I just need to move forward with *something*. It's OK if I don't impress child-me and my memories of my future love life. Lord knows my expectations were all screwed up on that front, anyway.

I mean, divorces really are chic now. You can reinvent yourself halfway through, which god knows people need.

I had a chat the other day with a seventy-year-old in the nut section of Whole Foods about aging and omega-3s. I made sure to mention a few times how spry he seemed, how glowing his skin. He broke down the real shit for me:

35–45 early middle age
45–55 middle middle age
55–65 late middle age
65–75 early old age
75–85 middle old age
85–95 late old age
> 95 quite elderly

So we're on the precipice.

It's more slippery to be on the precipice out here in the country. If I'm not fighting to survive on a subway platform every single minute, time goes faster. I am going to slide right into middle middle before I know it.

.

Matilda,

That's why it's important to have children and families, I think. To stay young.

.

Harry,

If I ever have a baby I'm naming it Moon Wisdom Goodman.

NO! I'm going to have twins like you and me except not just half this time and name them:

COBALT AND SAFFRON. The best two colors. The only colors.

Matilda,

I read an article today on the train about a woman who was hit in the head with a wayward ceiling fan. She had a total brain reboot; essentially starting life over—she had zero memories, zero sense of how to interact with the world. Before her accident she had been a wild child, swilling booze and driving too fast and marrying young. And afterward she was tempered, quiet—and, of course, pretty naïve. She literally had to start over. Twenty years later she enrolled in college (for the second time).

Odd to see such a clear reminder of the fact that we're all just a pile of cells and neurons, and if they are rearranged—well then, we change as well.

.

Harry,

Quite right.

You know what else?

John Wilkes Booth's brother saved Abraham Lincoln's son from sure death in a train accident.

Chills, right?

Robert Todd Lincoln. But it's not like Robert went on to be president or anything. Maybe he was another Roger Clinton. God, don't you just LOVE Roger Clinton? Even the thought of that guy makes me smile.

Matilda,

I'm going to find Vera and confront her.

.

Harry,

Really?

.

Matilda,

Do you think it will be a turn-off? Should I just give her space?

.

Matilda,

Helloooooo . . . where are you?

.

Harry,

I found Mom.

.

Matilda,

Really?? Where was she?!

Harry,

She was in the geranium section at her favorite greenhouse, the one halfway between home and Maine. I woke up yesterday at dawn and knew she was going to be there, as sure as I knew about that black Cabbage Patch doll named Maria.

The greenhouse she always made us stop at on our drive to camp—the one with the field of zinnias. The one that smells like rain-soaked dirt and growth and life and death and fish a little bit. (They have a sad koi pond in the middle with just a trickle of water. Not enough to be impressive, just to make you have to pee if you're standing next to it.)

So I got in the car and went. I was there by 8 a.m.

The greenhouse lady was standing in the geranium section, too, next to a big stack of pots—green, like jade, with symbols on them that looked Asian.

Mom sort of spooked when I saw her but in an "oh that was inevitable" way. Like a kid when you catch them in hide-and-seek. They're sort of relieved not to have to hide anymore?

She looked at me and kind of fluttered weakly and said, typically, "Oh . . . just one second, Matilda, I just have to go tinkle."

And then she turned and fled to the bathroom.

Didn't Mom spend our whole childhood having to pee? She said her pregnancy with us ruined her pelvic floor, but I guess she meant YOU, because I did not come out of her body. Because she is not my mother.

I'll tell you this, Harry: It is as though Mom has died, in a way, to me. And yet I love her more than ever.

In the movie version of this recap, I would storm to the bathroom and slam open the door and cry "MOM!!!!" in an adolescent sob, but would be answered only by the sad flapping of the torn window dressing playing in the breeze of an open pane, with the squeal of hybrid car tires in the background.

In real life I stormed to the bathroom and slammed open the door and cried "MOM!!!!" in an adolescent sob that surprised me with its vibrato and feeling.

And Mom said, "One second, Matilda, I'm just finishing up here."

It was a bathroom without stalls, so she said this to me from the actual toilet, which was low to the ground like a child's.

So I looked at her at that moment, Harry—I looked at her and waited to be annoyed. I usually am—about everything. Why can't she call tinkle pee like everyone else? Why can't she find a bra with an underwire? Why can't she be more proud of me?

So then she looks up from the child toilet (her knees are up high because the toilet's so close to the floor) and she says:

"Matilda, I just want you to know that I love you and I'm so proud of you."

And then I saw her for what she is. A lady who is doing her absolutely fucking best to love me. A lady who is scared, and who is trying very hard, a lady on a tiny toilet. Human, breakable, ridiculous.

A lady who did not give me her genetics after all. Her faults are not a personal insult to me, or tarot cards for my future. They are just regular person faults.

They are your faults, Harry, to be honest. The self-delusion and the fear. My future just broke wide open, Harry. Because I don't belong to any of you, anymore.

Well, except for Dad.

Talking points:

"It was a long time ago, Matilda."

"We made a decision to save our marriage and to make a family. And you came out of it, and it was such a gift."

"Dad had a sex addiction, which is a real thing. He made a huge transgression. And I stood by him, even though he's now forsaken me."

"You and Harry were always so fond of each other, it just seemed like fate, that you were born on the same day, just to different mothers."

"How could we let the baby be adopted by someone else? I never questioned that I was supposed to raise you."

"I'm reminded of my failures as a mother every day—but I've never been lacking in love."

"We gave you two everything, which is perhaps why you both have issues with entitlement, like the rest of your generation." (!)

To which I replied: "Well, your generation of women just pretended they were men in the name of feminism, and took PRIDE in having latchkey kids, which simply left us feeling abandoned and also frustrated because there were no lipstick samples to raid!"

And then I said, "I love you, Mom. I was really scared when you had cancer."

SO that's it, Harry. You're my half brother. Also, from Mom's understanding, my real mother is kind of a crack whore somewhere. And I'm guessing not a Jew. Not even a little.

·

Matilda,

Wow. IS this true? My god. I'm totally shocked. I mean . . . are you OK? We're not twins?

·

Harry,

Oh, quite. Isn't it funny after all this that Mom and Dad are big liars, too? The BIGGEST. Harry, I just thought of something.

·

Matilda,

What?

·

Harry,

Maybe that barmaid name story was true. Remember? How you're named after Dad's favorite Beatle and I'm named after his favorite barmaid?

.

Matilda,

Jesus Christ.

.

Harry,

It's OK, actually. My whole body is floating. I feel free, like I did right after I dropped the bucket on that horse. I don't have to conform to anything, because I don't belong to anything. I am a lone wolf. I can be bad. Lord knows my birth mother was. Who do you think she is? I guess we won't find out until the sequel.

.

Matilda,

Is Mom OK?

.

Harry,

I think she's in Maine somewhere. I don't know. I found a lot of Passover wine in the basement here, Harry. Viscous, never spoils.

I wish you were here. Any Vera news?

.

Matilda,

I haven't found her yet.

I did get some good news this morning, though. Seems unimportant now. But I'm a tenured professor. Set for life. I'll have to live in the country forever, I suppose.

.

Harry,

But that's amazing, Harry! It's what you wanted!

.

Matilda,

Yes, it is.

.

Harry,

I found some Willa Cather on my old bookshelf. More fitting than *Lolita,* so I switched books.

Here's the stuff:

I was entirely happy. Perhaps we feel like that when we die and become a part of something entire, whether it is sun and air, or goodness and knowledge. At any rate, that is happiness; to be dissolved into something complete and great.

I feel that way now, Harry. I really do. I'm going to embrace my new truths.

.

Matilda,

What is your new truth?

.

Harry,

Well for one, I am going to be a writer. A writer who takes wedding pictures sporadically, just for the love of it. I've finished my *Wedding Photographer* manuscript. It's a fucking masterpiece, naturally.

.

Matilda,

That's great, really. Hey—I wrote something for you.

Seventeen (You Wore Blue)

it amazes me still
how the pavement can sparkle with marcasite
down the ashen new york sidewalks
you wore blue
and tapped your feet not impatiently,

just for something to do.
in the 23rd row, 5th seat

we came from over 100 miles away
boys' choirs harmonized lushly
a soprano in the highest row
played herself to the dance of the song
voices sank in like almond oil smeared across my skin
yet the music did not move me
you adjusted your collar, flattened your hair,
ran a finger across your slick pink mouth
and I could not help but think
it is these things God notices,
the shine of a moistened lip,
the glimmer of glass upon a city street.

.

Harry,

I like that very much.

.

Matilda,

I found her.

She was in the karaoke joint in Chinatown. The one she'd tried
to drag me to after the reading, but at which I was too tired/too
distracted/too stuck in the mud to join her. I knew she'd be there. I
suspect she's there most nights—Vera loves nothing more than to
hear her own melodic voice at high volume. And why shouldn't she,
Matilda? She's resplendent. There's nothing she can't do.

My entrance into the karaoke place was Kubrick-worthy—a hidden entrance off a side street, three concrete steps down. Rain hard on the grates that are used for food market commerce all day long. The kind of grates I have a fear I'll fall through, being washed clean by the rain of cabbage or squid or hot sauce detritus.

A woman in front of a red velvet curtain manned the pin-drop-quiet entrance. She was wearing dark lipstick and nails and severe hair and appeared to have been waiting for me, but I couldn't get any words out exactly. I just motioned at the space behind her, and she parted the curtain.

A fifty-yard hallway of private rooms appeared, each entrance lit by a single spotlight in a sea of black lacquer. Doors covered in shiny red leather with little porthole windows which invite you to look inside and witness the raucous, sound-proofed action—each window a vignette, a mime of great enthusiasm, of joie de vive, of expensive drinking. I didn't know which room she was in, Matilda, or if she was even in one at all! So I looked through each porthole in turn. My shoes squeaked moisture on the floor.

There were college boys with beers singing metal tunes, there were middle-aged women with bright lips and ill-fitting tube tops, there were bodies draped and bodies seizing and some folks fighting and some people kissing. She was in the one about halfway down. I saw the back of her first; I recognized that red silk top.

I stopped cold at the window, my breath fogging the glass. She was with a few of her friends from work (lots of tortoiseshell and good if ironic hair, and champagne in each hand). She had the microphone and her head was tilted back and she seemed so *infected with joy.* I've never seen her quite like that—almost out of her body, still controlled but feral.

I tried to turn and leave before she saw me but she saw me. Actually, her friend in glasses said "Oh, shit" first, before she turned, but since I couldn't hear anything, it was more like *Ohhh, shittt,* silently mouthed in slow motion.

So then I walked in, and all the sound washed over me like a wave. And my ears were ringing a little bit and she touched my arm and I sat down so that she was standing, facing me, and my eyes were level with her stomach. And it was flat.

Her hand fluttered down. And then she sat down, too, and she said, "Oh god. I'm so sorry, Harry. I couldn't bring myself to tell you."

And I said: "You lost the baby?"

The room was sort of fuzzing and spinning and almost *kinetic* in the way it was in Wildwood when we drank Dad's Tanqueray and laughed at the ceiling all night, except this time it wasn't as funny and I'm not as young anymore.

And she said: "There never was a baby."

"What do you mean?"

"I tried, Harry. I tried to get pregnant so the fortune-teller would be right and we could be together. And I just *assumed* I would be pregnant soon enough without the birth control, so I just told you about it a little ahead of time! It was so cinematic and perfect, remember?

"But then it just didn't happen, the universe didn't behave, and . . . I guess it all just took on a life of its own. I never meant to hurt you. I tried to tell you—how the universe has many possibilities—with the Riemann sphere. But maybe I was too vague."

273

Matilda, here the room sort of slowed down and I saw Vera moving and talking verrrry slowwwly and I saw her as she truly is—not some sort of savant or savior or perfect human or my true love, but a young, *young half-formed* person. A person who does not benefit from the addition of me, and whom I do not benefit from the addition of.

"It *should* have been true—the universe *wanted* it to be true, and in another parallel universe it *was* true. Harry, do you think—do you think we could start over?"

"You know what, Vera? This is OK. This is fine. This *is better than fine.*"

"What? I'll make it up to you, Harry. I will. Let me just get my things and we'll go to my place to talk. You know—I feel quite relieved actually. We have this out in the open now. We can start again, Harry!"

Now Vera was gesticulating wildly and grabbing her things and knocking over some glasses in the process . . .

And I have to tell you, Matilda—while she was talking, and she kept talking—her words started to float farther and farther away from me, so that I couldn't even quite catch them, only snippets.

And instead of hearing her, I started instead to focus on the music that was playing, and it was Freddie Mercury. Matilda, it was the song, the song we both agree is the best song of all time—*our* song.

BOHEMIAN RHAPSODY

Is this the real life?
Is this just fantasy?

And I knew—I knew in that moment, it didn't matter what she had to say. I was free. I was fucking free, just like you are. She will be happier without me. But that's not the point.

.

Hey Harry,

Oh my god! Oh shit, Harry. I'm so sorry. I can't believe there's no baby! I really wanted that baby, Harry. I thought it would make us a family again. It was a fucking boy! I can't believe I was wrong.

.

Matilda,

You know what—I don't think I wanted that baby.

.

Harry,

What! But I thought you wanted to be a dad?

.

Matilda,

I do. Matilda, I should let you know that I contacted your dermatologist (I know all your passwords, naturally) and properly ended it for you. I told him you don't love him. He wasn't surprised. Said he hasn't heard from you in some time. He wishes you well.

Hey Harry,

What the fuck? Have you lost your mind, Harry? He was my
ONLY OPTION!

You have to fix this!

.

Matilda,

Gary is not your only option. He's a fucking terrible option, actually.

I also called the chair of my department and handed in my notice.

.

Harrison Goodman,

ARE YOU ON DRUGS????!!!!

.

Matilda,

Stop and listen to me, for once.

Pack a bag. I'm coming to get you.

Acknowledgments

So many people have helped Harry and Matilda come into being. I am deeply indebted to readers and supporters Judy Stein, David Hirschman, Sara Goldsmith, Kara Canal, Jane Spencer, Lindsay Foehrenbach, Joslyn Hansen, Kate Stonebraker, Becky Dorf, Hannah Garrison, Sarah Hirschman, Catherine Choudhry, Manjari Sharma, Jackie Delamatre, Carrie Bancroft, Theresa Ganz, Jen Snow, Derek Delahunt, Jennifer Salcido, Manya Rubenstein, Clay Rockefeller, Emily Steffian, Charles Hulin, the Hirschman Family, Ken Dardick, Terence Keegan, Flannery Patton, Lauren Cerand, Brian Clamp, Maggie Riggs, Nathan Deuel, Joe Caliguire, Yvette Koch, Stephen Pierson, Emma Dries, and Tara Kole.

Special thanks Cody Curran for her continued magic and inspiration, to Nadia Sawicki for lending me words for Harry, and to Ari Lubet for his extreme goodness.

Much appreciation to Rebecca Friedman for championing Harry and Matilda from their humble beginnings, and to the inspired Jenny Jackson for believing in them and making them better.

Deepest thanks to my family.

A Note About the Author

Rachel Hulin is a writer and photographer. Her writing has appeared in *Rolling Stone, Nerve, Radar, The Huffington Post,* and *The Daily Beast.* Her photography book, *Flying Henry,* was published in 2013. Hulin has a BA from Brown University and an MA from NYU. She lives with her husband and two children in Providence, Rhode Island.